By Ellie Boswell

THE WITCH OF TURLINGHAM ACADEMY
UNDERCOVER MAGIC

THE WITCH OF TURLINGHAM ACADEMY

UNDERCOVER MAGIC

ELLIE BOSWELL

www.atombooks.net/tween

ATOM

First published in Great Britain in 2012 by Atom

A CIP catalogue record for this book
is available from the British Library.

ISBN 978-1-907410-96-3

Typeset in Minion by M Rules

Printed and bound in Great Britain by
Clays Ltd, St Ives plc

Papers used by Atom are from well-managed forests
and other responsible sources.

MIX
Paper from
responsible sources
FSC® C104740
www.fsc.org

Atom
An imprint of
Little, Brown Book Group
100 Victoria Embankment
London EC4Y 0DY

An Hachette UK Company
www.hachette.co.uk

www.atombooks.net/tween

With special thanks to Leila Rasheed

ONE

Sophie Morrow groaned and pulled the duvet over her head as the house filled with clattering and noise. There was no way it was time to get up!

'It's Sunday, Mum!' she called through a huge yawn. 'Go back to bed!'

The noise continued and Sophie realised it wasn't her mother moving about. It was someone hammering on the front door.

She scrambled up, dragging a hand through her messy hair, and ran downstairs. A familiar face was pressed against the frosted glass panel.

'Katy!' She flung it open. Her best friend grinned at her, pale cheeks flushed with the autumn chill and her black hair half-hidden under a woolly hat.

'Sophie, come on out!' she said. 'The last of the leaves finally fell off the trees last night and we're mucking round in them – Callum's there!' She blushed. 'Oh, and some of the other boys are, too.'

'Cool! Give me a second to get dressed.' Sophie turned, but Katy caught her arm.

'Wait … I made you a little present,' she said, reaching into her coat pocket. 'I'd really like you to wear it.'

She handed Sophie a friendship bracelet, plaited together with a rainbow of coloured threads. Charms in the shape of flowers and fruit were worked into it – an ivy-leaf, a bunch of cherries and a cute red tomato.

Sophie drew in her breath. 'Oh, Katy, thanks!' She laid it against her wrist, so the charms caught the light.

'You like it?' Katy asked.

'Like it? I love it!' Sophie stroked the ivy leaf. 'And

the charms are perfect. Did you choose leaves and fruit because ...?' She tailed off, not wanting to mention the word *magic* aloud, just in case someone was listening.

Katy nodded. 'Because of your ... green fingers.' Their eyes met and Sophie knew they were both thinking the same thing: Sophie was a witch, and witch powers came from the great forces of nature.

'It's the best present in the world,' she said, throwing her arms round Katy.

'Well, you're the best friend in the world, so you deserve it!' Katy said with a laugh. 'I made one for me, too, exactly the same.' She held up her wrist.

'So cool!' Sophie clapped her hands. 'It's like we're twins.' She noticed Katy's cheeks flush. 'I mean, obviously we look totally different and, um, our families are sworn mortal enemies, but, y'know ...'

They laughed together. Katy came from a family of witch hunters. They'd only found out how different they were after they'd become friends, and now nothing was going to become between them – not even witch hunting.

'The bracelets aren't identical,' Sophie added, examining the bracelets side by side. 'Yours hasn't got this bunch of cherries—'

'Oh! I almost forgot,' Katy took Sophie's friendship bracelet and flipped it over so the charms were reversed. The bunch of cherries had a piece of metal attached to the back. 'This one's special – it's really a fridge magnet.'

'Katy, that's so clever,' Sophie exclaimed, realising what it meant. Magnets blocked a witch's powers, making Sophie just like any other human. If she wore it one way, it was just a pretty bracelet. As soon as the magnet came in contact with her skin, it could save her life.

'When the bracelet's reversed, your powers will be hidden from any witch hunter,' Katy said. She hesitated, then added: 'Even my family.'

'Thanks, Katy!' Sophie hugged her again. It wasn't easy being best friends with a witch hunter – if Katy's family ever found out Sophie was a witch, they would both be in danger. But it was worth the risk, she thought. *I've never had a better friend.*

'You're welcome.' Katy hugged her back. 'Now hurry up and get dressed so we can go and find the others!'

Sophie raced up the stairs to her bedroom, the charms on the bracelet catching the dim sunrays as she went.

Sophie followed Katy past the big windows of the new science block and into the courtyard. Turlingham School loomed above them, turrets and towers casting spiky shadows across the concrete. She saw her friends on the other side of the courtyard, shouting and laughing as they chased after Mark, who was carrying Erin in a piggyback across the grass, weaving in and out of the trees.

'Mark, slow down!' Erin shrieked in her American accent, between giggles. 'You're going to drop me, I swear!' The gulls overhead echoed her squeals.

'Hey, Soph!' Tall, curly-haired Callum waved to her. Sophie waved back. She'd known Callum for what seemed like for ever – her mother and his father were joint head teachers at Turlingham Academy.

'Look! No hands!' Erin yelled, waving to Sophie –

then she lost her balance and slid off into a big pile of leaves with a whoop of laughter. Mark fell down next to her. Sophie ran over to them as the others crowded round, giggling and tossing armfuls of leaves on top of Erin and Mark.

'Hey, you two, stop kissing under there!' Kaz laughed as she chucked some more.

'Yeah, can't you keep your hands off each other for a second?' Katy added as she and Sophie reached them.

Sophie laughed. She knew Erin loved to be the centre of attention with Mark – and Erin seemed so happy to be finally going out with him!

Mark scrambled up out of the leaves, blushing and frowning.

'Hey, Mark, are you OK?' Sophie asked. 'We were only joking . . .'

'Yeah, course I'm OK!' Mark muttered. He ran off and joined the other boys who were hanging out under the trees.

'Oh no, did we upset him?' Lauren said, looking worried. 'We didn't mean to!'

Erin got to her feet, her cheeks red with embarrassment. 'The thing is,' she whispered, beckoning the girls in, 'don't tell him I told you, but ... we haven't actually kissed yet.'

'Wha-at?' Kaz's mouth dropped open. 'But he's so into you!'

'Yeah!' Joanna looked puzzled. 'And you've been going out for a whole two weeks!'

'I know.' Erin's mouth turned down. 'I'm worried he doesn't like me any more.'

'As if!' Sophie replied. 'Erin, he's head over heels. Anyone can see that.'

'I hope you're right.' Erin sighed.

'We are! Come on – you're not allowed to mope about something so silly,' Sophie said, putting on a stern voice. 'Or you'll get ... ' she ducked to scoop up an armful of leaves, '... leaf bombed!' She hurled them at Erin, who shrieked and laughed and tried to hide behind Katy. Sophie dodged as Erin scooped up more to fight back with – and gasped as Lauren cheekily tossed handfuls over her head.

Kaz grabbed a big bunch of leaves and darted over

to the group of boys. Before Callum could react, she shoved them down the back of his jumper.

'Urgh! I'll get you for that!' Callum roared in mock anger. He scooped up more leaves and flung them at Kaz, who squealed in delight. Then a gust of tangy, salty wind blew in from the sea and suddenly all the leaves were swirling and dancing round.

Sophie grabbed some leaves out of the air, ran over to the boys and flung her armful at them.

'Girls against boys – leaf wars!' she cried.

'You're on!' Oliver Campbell, a quiet boy with a big, friendly smile, dashed forward and threw more leaves at Kaz. The others joined in.

'Oh no, I'm getting out of here!' Lauren giggled. She ducked for shelter behind the biggest oak tree. Kaz and Oliver dived round to join her.

Sophie looked up into the maze-like branches of the oak tree and saw a flash of glossy black fur. It was Gally – her squirrel familiar. She winked at him, and Gally, catching on at once, darted round the tree, shaking the branches. Kaz, Lauren and Oliver yelled as they were covered in leaves.

'Oh, look at that squirrel! It's so close!' Oliver shouted, pointing as Gally scampered away like a streak of black lightning. Kaz and Oliver chased after him, but Gally disappeared into the woods.

Sophie watched, laughing.

Katy nudged her. 'Hey – it wasn't *you* who made the leaves fall last night, was it?' she whispered, her eyes wide.

Sophie laughed again and shook her head. 'I wish my powers were that strong!' she whispered back. 'Nope, it's not magic – just autumn, same as every year.'

'Let's go and explore the woods!' Kaz yelled in the distance. The others followed her towards the trees that bordered the school.

Sophie held Katy back, and they brushed the leaves off each other. Looking up, Sophie noticed that Callum was still there, shifting from foot to foot as he gazed at Katy. 'What's up, Callum?' Sophie asked him.

'Oh . . . I – er – I just wanted to apologise to Katy for getting leaves all over her.' Callum rubbed one Converse shyly against the other.

'Oh, Callum! That's the point of a leaf battle!' Sophie teased.

Callum ignored her and came up to Katy. 'Are you OK?' he said, gazing deep into her green eyes.

Katy blushed. 'Oh ... yeah! Of course!' She flicked a golden leaf out of her hair. 'Are you? OK, I mean?'

Sophie rolled her eyes. She wished they would just hurry up and get together. Hoping that if she left them in peace Callum would get to the point, she ran off after the others.

Sophie caught up with Kaz and noticed her glance back at Callum and Katy. Sophie's smile faltered. *Oh no, Kaz has a crush on Callum, too.* But he was so obviously into Katy – in fact, he might even be making his move that very minute ...

'So, uh, I got to level sixteen on Elfin Warriors,' Callum's voice drifted over to them, 'and now I have the secret key and forty-two extra Druid Skill Points!'

'Oh, um ... wow,' Katy's puzzled voice replied.

Kaz looked relieved, and Sophie groaned to herself. Callum was a great friend, but he was never going to get anywhere with chat-up lines like that!

Sophie felt a pebble dig into her foot. 'Ouch! You guys go on, I'll be there in a sec,' she called.

Sophie sat down on a stump and began unlacing her trainer, while her friends ran on into the woods. She tipped the stone out of her shoe and sat for a moment, enjoying the still peace and the power of nature that she could feel all around her. The wind moaned through the trees and Sophie smiled to herself. But her face fell when she heard a voice from behind her.

'Nice morning for hunting witches!'

Sophie jumped up and spun round, her heart beating fast. The boy who stood scowling on the path was as handsome as Katy was pretty, and he had the same black hair and green eyes. But Sophie knew Ashton Gibson was nothing like his kind, gentle sister.

'Ashton,' she said cautiously. In the distance, she could hear her friends calling to each other as they ran through the woods. If she screamed for them, she thought, they'd come – but then Ashton would know for sure she had something to hide. He had seen her save Katy's life with a spell just a few weeks ago, and he was furious that he hadn't managed to prove to his family of witch hunters that Sophie was a witch.

Ashton stepped forward, his feet crunching in the frost. His hand was clenched in his blazer pocket.

Sophie instinctively backed away. *What's he got in there?*

He pulled out his fist, grey dust spilling between his fingers. Iron filings, the easiest way for a witch hunter to find witches. They were treated with a witch hunters' potion, designed to form into the shape of a crescent moon in the presence of a witch.

'Take that!' Ashton threw the iron filings.

Sophie barely had time to duck before the tiny pieces of iron scattered over her. Her mouth tasted sour with terror as she realised she was in big, big trouble. The iron filings fell on the floor and Sophie looked down, expecting to see the shape that would seal her fate. Except she didn't. The filings scattered and were lost on the muddy path. Sophie gasped, caught between confusion and relief.

Ashton stared at the ground, a frown of confusion

on his face. 'How the …? I *know* you're a witch!' he burst out.

Sophie relaxed as she remembered her friendship bracelet. The magnet was touching her skin, protecting her.

'What do you think you're doing, Ashton?' she demanded, trying to look puzzled as well as outraged. 'First you call me a witch – that's so rude! – and then you throw stuff at me?! That could have gone in my eyes!'

Ashton's mouth hardened. 'I don't know how you're beating the test,' he said. 'But I *do* know you're a witch. I'll catch you out one day. You can't make *me* look stupid.'

He strode away.

As soon as his back was turned, Sophie checked that her friends couldn't see her from where they were and she flipped her bracelet round. She rubbed the crescent moon ring that she always wore – it was her Source, the origin of her magic. Tingling energy rushed through her, and the wind roared through the trees, as if it was strengthening her power. Silvery willow leaves swirled down and danced around her. Sophie felt a smile come to her lips as the ring glowed as pale as the frost on the ground.

'Forces of the earth,' she whispered, 'rise up!'

A huge gust of wind rushed through the clearing and tossed a huge drift of muddy leaves up into the air. Ashton cried out in disgust as they blew right into his face. He spun round, trying to beat them off, tripped on a root and went over, flailing his arms – *splash!* – into a puddle.

'You're right, Ashton – you definitely don't need me to make you look stupid!' Sophie said with a cheeky grin. Then she turned to join her friends. She didn't fancy staying round to face Ashton's anger. But as soon as she started to move, she heard a scream ring out from her left.

It was Kaz's voice – and it was the scream of someone in pain . . .

TWO

Sophie burst through the trees, jumping over logs and fallen branches. She found her friends in a small clearing, clustered together.

'What happened?! What's the matter?' Sophie pushed through the group. She looked down to see Kaz sitting on the ground, her face white and tear-streaked. Joanna crouched next to her with one arm round her shoulders.

Joanna looked up. 'She tripped and hurt her ankle.'

Kaz gave a wobbly smile as Sophie dropped down next to them. 'Don't worry, I'll be fine.'

But Sophie could see there was blood coming through her sock.

'She tripped on this.' Oliver pointed to a patch of earth a few metres away. There was a large, rusty grating set into the ground. The vertical and horizontal bars locked together into a complex, inter-weaving pattern of ironwork. A huge padlock secured it.

Callum walked over to look and put his hand on the vent. 'Air's coming through. Maybe it's part of the school ventilation system.'

'I don't know what it is,' Sophie said, 'but I do know you'd better get to the nurse, Kaz! Can you stand up?'

Kaz winced as she climbed to her feet and tried to put weight on her ankle.

'I think I might need someone to lean on.' She glanced at Callum hopefully.

'I'll help!' Oliver rushed to support her.

'Um, thanks,' said Kaz, sounding slightly annoyed. 'Oliver might need some help though, so if anyone else would like to volunteer?'

'No problem, Kaz,' Callum said cheerfully. 'Here, give me your hand. Olly, you take her other one ... '

Sophie grinned as Kaz headed back towards the school, beaming all over her face with a boy on each arm.

Sophie pushed open the door of the library, wincing as the noise hit her – the rumble of fifty Year 9s all talking at the same time. The school week seemed to have gone so fast, the bandage had come off Kaz's ankle, and it was hard to believe it was already Friday morning and time to start their extended history project.

'Sophie!' Katy waved from her perch on the windowsill. Sophie squeezed through the crowd to join her, avoiding elbows and folders being waved wildly.

'Great choice of seat!' she said, boosting herself up onto the windowsill. She looked out across the packed library. It was a huge, sprawling room, full of old-fashioned bookcases made out of dark wood. Big stone columns held up the vaulted roof, and the iron vents set into the floor meant that the many nooks and corners were always full of strange draughts.

Katy pointed up at the bookcase next to them. 'Hey, have you ever seen these carvings running along the tops of the bookcases? They're so sweet – little mice and squirrels and birds.'

Sophie smiled. 'I know, I love—'

'Year 9! Quieten down!' A hairy hand belonging to Mr McGowan, their history teacher, waved above the sea of uniforms. The room grew quieter, and he went on: 'I'm thrilled that you're so fired-up about your family history project—'

Sophie was suddenly listening hard. *Family* history?

Mr McGowan went on: 'It is compulsory, and it will be good practice for your GCSE coursework next year. But it should be lots of fun, too!'

Erin, who was backed against a pillar with Lauren next to her, put her hand up. 'Um, I don't get it. What exactly do we have to do?'

He held up a sheaf of hand-outs. 'These explain everything!' he said, passing them round. 'First you'll be using websites and books to discover who your ancestors were, and then you'll be interviewing other people in your year to find out about their families.'

Sophie took a hand-out as the boy in front passed them back to her. The paper was headed with a question: *What secrets lurk in YOUR family history?*

Sophie gulped. She and Katy knew exactly what secrets lurked in their family histories! Katy's family were all witch hunters, and Sophie's family on her dad's side were witches. If anyone found out, both of them would be at risk.

The hand-out trembled in her hands, and Sophie quickly put it down before anyone noticed. She glanced over at Katy, who was staring at the paper, looking slightly sick. She looked up and caught Sophie's eye. Sophie knew they were both thinking the same thing: they couldn't get out of doing the project, but they couldn't tell the truth, either. They would have to think of a solution – and fast.

Sophie pulled a book from the shelf and pretended to examine it. She shot a glance at the clock. It was only ten minutes till lunch and she still hadn't thought of a way of getting round the project. Erin was passing a note to Lauren, and Joanna and Kaz were giggling as they doodled on each other's notepads. She breathed out. It seemed no one was taking the project too seriously. Maybe they would be lucky.

Katy was sitting in an alcove at one of the computers. Sophie slid into the seat next to her. 'How's it going?' she whispered.

'Ssssshhhh!' came a furious hiss. Sophie jumped. The Head Prefect, Maggie Millar, with an armful of books, scowled down at them. 'Some of us have real GCSE coursework to do!' she snapped.

'Sorry, Maggie,' said Sophie hastily. Katy stifled a giggle as Maggie walked on. Sophie was about to ask her if she'd managed to make up some good stories about her family's past when Callum came through the door. Sophie waved. He grinned and came over and sat next to her, giving Katy a shy smile.

'I'm way behind on my coursework,' he told them. He glanced at the clock. 'But it's hardly worth starting before lunch – I'll just check the Elfin Warriors site.'

Sophie pulled a sour face. 'I am shocked and appalled at your behaviour, Callum Pearce,' she growled, making her voice tremble with irritation like Maggie's. 'You will never get good GCSE grades if you procrastinate like this!'

Katy grinned.

'Yeah, very funny.' Callum tapped away at the computer and then frowned at the screen. 'Hmm, can you think of another word for hero?' Callum asked. 'I've been stuck on this one for days, and I can't unlock the secret level without it. Messy deal for hero? It's got 4 letters.'

Sophie laughed. 'Don't try and suck me into your geeky game!'

'It's really good,' Callum protested. 'The Elfin warrior has to—'

'Um . . . ' Katy cleared her throat. 'Another word for hero is lead, isn't it? Like the lead in a film.'

Callum looked back at the screen, where his elf character was waiting patiently in front of closed stone doors. 'Hey, Katy, that's brilliant! Lead's an anagram for deal – a messy deal. Good one.' He typed in the word and hit return. The stone doors grated open and the elf ran through. 'Thanks!'

Sophie grinned at Katy. Katy ducked her head and turned pink, but she was smiling.

A second later, Sophie jumped as the electric bell drilled through the air. The library broke out in a racket of laughter and conversation and scraping chairs as girls and boys scrambled up from their seats and headed for the door. Callum piled his books into his bag. 'Coming to lunch?' he asked.

'We'll see you down there,' Sophie told him. Callum waved and joined the rush for the door.

Katy was staring towards the far side of the library. Sophie followed her gaze . . . and saw Ashton, standing by a column, idly leafing through a book.

'I have to talk to Ashton,' Katy whispered to Sophie. 'We'll be changing a lot of background information on our families for the project so whatever I write he'll have to back it up or we'll be found out!'

Sophie watched as Katy went across the library and tapped Ashton on the shoulder. They moved towards the patch of sun that fell through a skylight, their heads close together. Sophie felt a clutch of fear. She didn't like seeing Katy talking to Ashton; she knew how dangerous he was. She concentrated on hearing their words.

'You've got to help me,' Katy was saying, looking up at him. 'If anyone asks you'll have to back me up.'

Ashton shrugged. 'Sort it out yourself,' he replied coldly. 'You're supposed to be the perfect one, aren't you?'

He pushed past her, but then suddenly turned back. Glancing round as if to check there was no one in hearing distance, he leaned close in to hiss: 'Just make sure you find out about Sophie Morrow's family. I know what she really is – and so do you.'

Katy flicked her gaze towards Sophie. She said firmly: 'Just leave her alone. You were proved wrong just a few weeks ago, remember.'

Ashton glared at Sophie. Sophie dropped her gaze and started putting her books into her bag, hands trembling. She heard Ashton hiss: 'I'm ashamed of you, Katy – you're acting as if it doesn't mean anything to be a Gibson! What do you think Mum and Dad would do if I told them you were fraternising with one of *them*?'

Sophie trembled again, but this time with rage. Ashton was such a bully! She glanced up to the skylight above him. It was half-covered in leaves. She clenched her fists and muttered: 'Earth, water, wind and fire. Forces of the earth, blow that window open.'

A sudden gust of wind whipped through the library, scattering papers. Students squealed. The skylight rattled as the wind hit it, then fell open, tipping its load of leaves straight over Ashton's head.

'Gross!' Ashton batted at the damp, half-rotten leaves in his hair.

Katy clapped a hand to her mouth to cover her giggle. The other pupils turned round in surprise, then burst out laughing.

The librarian, Miss Haverstock, looked up from her computer. 'Ashton Gibson! What do you think you're doing, opening that skylight? Get out of here at once and clean yourself up!' she exclaimed.

Ashton rushed from the room, his face furious.

Sophie hid a grin, but as she finished packing her

history books away, she couldn't help feeling uneasy. OK, she'd scored over Ashton twice in a row – but he was really angry now. How long could her run of good luck last?

THREE

'Sophie, where's your Art folder?' Lauren said as they reached the canteen.

'Oh, duh!' Sophie stopped dead. 'I always forget that thing – don't know how, it's huge!'

She headed back to the library, against the flow of hungry students hurrying towards the canteen. As she turned the corner, the crowd thinned until she was striding down a deserted corridor, her footsteps loud in the silence. Display cabinets full of shields and cups lined the walls, casting shadows between them. One of the shadows seemed to detach itself from the wall and loom towards her.

Sophie gasped and did a double take as Ashton stepped out of the darkness. He blocked her way.

Sophie stopped, her heart beating fast.

'Hello, Sophie.' Ashton smiled coldly. 'You don't mind if I ask you a few questions, do you?'

'Questions?'

'About your family.' He added: 'Katy asked me to do her family history questionnaire, and you know how much I care about my sister.'

Liar! Sophie thought. 'Sorry, Ashton, I'm going to lunch.' She made to move past him, but Ashton moved to block her. She swallowed.

'What's the rush?' Ashton stepped in front of her. 'Can't you wait just a second?'

'No, I can't,' Sophie replied, and dodged past him.

He touched her on the shoulder and spun her round to look at him. 'Look, you convince me your family is normal, and I'll leave you alone for good.'

Sophie sighed. Ashton had been bugging her ever since the Welcome Back Dance; the idea that he would leave her alone was far-fetched . . . but worth a shot. 'OK. Fine,' she told him. 'What do you want to know?'

Ashton pulled out a black leather bound notebook and a fountain pen. Both had a gold monogram – G for Gibson – stamped on them.

Sophie took the opportunity to fiddle with her bracelet so the magnet was touching her skin.

'So,' he said, staring at her thoughtfully, 'tell me about your . . . grandparents. Were any of them special in any way?'

Sophie gave him a smile so false it made her teeth ache. 'Actually, my mum's dad was a captain in the Royal Navy. He went all over the world.' It was true. Nothing witchy about Grandad Morrow.

Ashton flicked open the book and made a note, smiling faintly.

Sophie watched nervously as the pen scratched over the paper.

'Good . . . very good. What about your other grandparents?' He edged towards her as he spoke. Sophie found herself stepping backwards and to the side. She put her Art folder in front of her like a defence, her heart thumping uncomfortably.

'M-my mum's mum was a nurse.' She felt Ashton's green eyes trained on her as the pen scratched like a claw.

'And your parents? Do they have any, er, talents?'

'Um …' Sophie took another step back and bumped into one of the display cabinets. Ashton glided across to stand right in front of her. He had amazingly long eyelashes. She blurted out: 'My mum can juggle. And she's a brilliant headmistress at this boarding school called Turlingham Academy … maybe you've heard of it. Is that the kind of thing you mean?'

'Not exactly,' Ashton murmured. He placed a hand on the cabinet either side of her and leaned in close. 'Why don't you just tell me *everything* about your family?'

Sophie swallowed. 'I … I've told you. I'm boring. I mean,' she hastily corrected herself, 'we're boring. Um …'

'Oh, I'm sure you're not.' Ashton had a smile in his voice. 'What about your father's relations?'

'I don't know them,' Sophie said, trying to keep her voice steady. 'He left when I was little.' *Because witch hunters like you were trying to capture him.*

Ashton hesitated. For a second, Sophie thought he might back off.

'So you've not met *anyone* on your father's side of the family?' he said, his face hardening.

Sophie's thoughts jumped to the only member of her father's family that she had met. Her grandma – a witch, persecuted and demagicked by witch hunters and sent to an institution because her insistence that witches exist made people think she was crazy. 'N-no. I've not met her,' Sophie said, the image of Grandma still strong in her mind. Then she winced. She'd said *her*. She looked up at Ashton, hoping he hadn't noticed. But, by the delighted expression on his face, she could tell that he had.

Ashton leaned back a little and Sophie took her chance. She ducked under his arm and backed out into the middle of the corridor.

'So, um,' she said, pulling out her own questionnaire in a desperate attempt to take the attention away from herself, 'you don't mind if I ask you about your family, too, do you?'

Ashton spun round to face her and looked startled. Then he smiled. 'Why not? *I've* got nothing to hide.' He folded his arms and leaned against the wall. 'The male line of the Gibsons has been tracked all the way back to the time of William the Conqueror. The earliest mention of our family is in the Doomsday Book.'

Sophie raised her eyebrows. 'That's ... impressive,' she said, not sure whether to believe him or not.

Ashton shrugged. 'It's important. I've had to memorise my family tree ever since I could speak.' He added: 'Want to hear it? It's my party trick.'

'Um ... go on then,' said Sophie, unable to hide her curiosity.

'The first true Gibson was Robert Giscard Gibson. He was the father of William Gibson, who was the father of Archibald Gibson, who was the father of Edmund Gibson, who was the father of Matthew Gibson, who was the father of ...'

Several minutes later, Ashton finished, '... and then

there are our second cousins, the Lloyd family: Miranda and Heather.'

Sophie, feeling slightly dizzy, could think of nothing to say but: 'Wow.'

Ashton was smiling – a warm smile that reached his eyes. Sophie couldn't help but smile back. Ashton reached for the chain round his neck. From it hung a pendant: a silver bar. He dangled the pendant in front of Sophie; it turned lazily on the chain.

'Is that a – er – family heirloom?' Sophie asked, watching it nervously.

'Kind of,' said Ashton. This time his smile was definitely not warm. 'We know it as the Witch Hunter's Bloodhound.'

Sophie stared as it swung back and forth like a compass needle. 'So, it's a good luck charm.'

'It's better than just luck. We Gibsons are very good at what we do,' Ashton murmured, his eyes on the bar. 'We *always* get our prey.'

Sophie was still feeling dizzy, and the turning needle didn't help. She found herself following it with her eyes, drawn towards it. Perhaps it was some kind of hypnotism trick. She decided not to stay and find out.

'I-I've got to go,' she stammered. Then she turned and ran.

As Sophie reached the library, she glanced back. Ashton was following her, his face furious. She slipped in through the doors and hurried on tiptoe to the bookshelves. The library was almost deserted. At the bottom of the aisle, she turned the corner and flattened herself against the end of the bookcase. Her heart felt as loud as a bass drum in her chest. She heard the library doors swing open again and footsteps come in, then pause. Sophie held her breath.

Long moments passed. Sophie breathed out, gently, and risked a glance round the corner of the bookcase. A Year-7 boy started and looked at her wide-eyed. Sophie put a finger to her lips and ducked into the next row of bookshelves. A floorboard creaked and she froze halfway down. The next moment, Ashton strode, frowning, past the end of the aisle. He didn't see her.

Sophie edged to the end of the aisle and ran on tiptoe in the opposite direction to him. With a careful look left and right, she slipped into the next row of bookcases. At the end of it was a wall, lined with doors to some private study rooms. Sophie glanced up and down the wall. At the far end, there was a smaller door labelled Rare Volumes Room.

Sophie ran to the door and tried the handle. It opened. She ducked in and shut the door gently behind her, then leaned against it and breathed out a sigh of relief.

Sophie gazed round, her nose wrinkling at the smell of old books. The room was small and shaped like a hexagon, with a bookcase in the centre stuffed with ancient-looking tomes, a sash window high on one wall and an old iron radiator under it. It didn't seem to be giving out much heat; the room was full of chilly draughts, just like the rest of the library.

Wondering how long she'd have to wait for Ashton to go away, Sophie headed for the radiator. She stuck her hands down the back of it to try and get some more heat, but the metal was icy cold.

Her fingers touched something hard. She fished it out and brushed the dust and cobwebs off.

'Cool . . . ' she murmured.

It was an old book, bound in leather, and held together by intricate bronze clasps. Sophie squinted at them; they looked almost like devilish little grinning faces. But although the binding was impressive, the cover was completely blank.

'There must be a title,' she muttered, turning it over and over. Suddenly she felt a tingle in her fingertips. She almost dropped the book in shock. The tingling rushed through her fingers and up her arms.

'Oh!' she gasped. It was the very same feeling she'd had when she put her Source on for the first time. *This book must be magic!*

She quickly turned her friendship bracelet over. As soon as the magnet left her skin, the cover blossomed with words:

'Magic Most Dark,' Sophie read with a shiver.

She took a deep breath, slowly lifted the edge of the cover – and slammed it shut again as a piercing whistle shot through her ears. She dropped the book and covered her ears with her hands but the noise was just as loud.

It faded after a second. Sophie sighed with relief. She hurried to the door and listened, wondering if it had been some kind of fire alarm. But there was no noise from outside. *Maybe I imagined it,* she thought.

Cautiously, she opened the book once more. The spine creaked and the pages were brittle. To her disappointment she saw the pages were blank. But then, under her gaze, words started to appear as if they were soaking into the page from the air.

'*A Spell That Shall Fox and Bewilder . . .*' she read, frowning as she tried to make out the strange, rambling script. It looped and criss-crossed the page so she sometimes had to turn the book sideways to make it out.

'*A Formula to Start a Fire . . .*' She flipped the page again. '*A Conjuration that Will Make Your Heart Harden . . . A Potion to Mislead Enemies . . .*' she read aloud. She skimmed down the pages, reading the lists of ingredients and equipment: phoenix blood, elephant tears, ambivalent acid, salts of magnesia . . .

Not all of the contents were spells. Some clearly relied on the power of nature, like the spells she had cast herself – but others asked for crucibles and tongs and strange ingredients ... in fact, she realised, they sounded like the mixtures and formulas that witch hunters created.

'*A Formula to Produce Phantom Effects*,' she read on – then faltered as she saw the title of the next spell. '*A Spell to Find Any Named Witch!*'

Sophie shuddered. *Any Named Witch*, she thought. She couldn't help but imagine what might happen if witch hunters got their hands on that spell. If they used it to find her father ... or her grandma ... or herself ...

The door behind her creaked. Sophie jumped and turned round, hiding the book behind her back just as Ashton pushed the door open.

'*There* you are,' Ashton said. His eyes scanned her and then the room. 'I knew you were up to something!'

Sophie backed against the radiator. There was no way she was going to let him see the magic book. She looked round for some kind of distraction. The bookshelf behind him was over-stuffed with books: they could fall at any moment . . .

Behind her back, Sophie rubbed her Source. She dropped her head, her hair falling in front of her face so Ashton couldn't see her lips moving, and muttered under her breath, 'Forces of the Earth – blow the books down!'

She shivered as energy rushed through her. The windows rattled as the draughts in the room swept together and blew towards the bookshelves. The books slid off the shelf and crashed to the ground.

'Ow!' Ashton threw up his hands to defend himself as books bounced off his head and shoulders.

Sophie pushed *Magic Most Dark* back down behind the radiator, then rushed past Ashton, jumping over the fallen books. Ashton made a grab for her but she dodged.

'I know you did that!' he shouted after her.

Sophie raced for the exit, her heart pounding. She would have to come back and study the book when Ashton was safely out of the way.

FOUR

'We're home, Mum!' Sophie called as she ran up the stairs to her bedroom, Katy close behind her. She threw open her bedroom door and dumped her bag on the floor, then scrambled onto the bed to pin up a curling corner of one of her Jareth Quinn posters. She turned back to Katy, who was closing the door behind her. 'Great – now we can talk!'

'Yes, what's all this about a magic book?' Katy joined Sophie on the beanbags under the window.

Sophie explained quickly. Katy listened, her eyes wide with amazement.

'A book of magic, at Turlingham Academy!' she said thoughtfully. 'I wonder how it got there?'

'I've no idea,' said Sophie. She'd been wondering the same thing all day. 'Let's go in the library and look for it again tomorrow. No one will be in there on a Saturday.'

'Definite plan,' Katy agreed.

Gally popped his head over the edge of the bean-bags. He had been playing in Sophie's jewellery box and had a necklace draped over one ear. The girls laughed, and Sophie gently took the necklace off him. Gally scampered over to Katy and laid a gold earring in her hand.

'Thanks, Gally, but that's Sophie's!' Katy said. She held up the earring, examining it closely. It was a slim hoop of gold with an enamelled daisy hanging from it. 'This is gorgeous, Sophie! Is it real gold?'

'Yes! I had to save up for them for ages, but they were so worth it.' Sophie searched for the other and put it next to the one Katy held, admiring the way they sparkled as they dangled.

Her mum called up the stairs: 'Girls! I hope you're getting on with your History project.'

Sophie groaned, and put the earrings away. 'I suppose we ought to!'

'This is such a nightmare,' Katy said as she fetched her History folder.

'I know,' Sophie agreed. 'I think I managed to bluff it today, but we've got to draw a family tree and hand it in! How am I going to do that without mentioning anyone on my father's side of the family?'

'We'll just have to make up some relatives for you,' Katy said. She grinned. 'I've always wanted to be related to someone interesting. Like, I don't know ... a spy. Or, no – a lion tamer!'

Sophie giggled. 'Hey, I think I'll put that in.' In her rough book, she added a great-great-uncle to the Poulter side of her family tree. 'Alexander Hedbitoff, lion tamer to the Tsar.'

Katy laughed.

'You know what would be really good,' said Sophie, studying her family tree, 'would be to have some rich relations, so I could have a fortune left to me or something.' She pulled her laptop towards her and quickly Googled. 'Here: Lord Kinver of Kettleby Magna. He's got a huge family – he won't notice one extra.' She added him in as a relative on her father's side.

'Sophie! What if he finds out?' Katy giggled.

Sophie shrugged. 'I *might* be related to him, for all I know.'

Katy went quiet and tipped her head to one side. 'You must be curious about them,' she said eventually.

'Of course! I don't know any of the Poulters – well, apart from Grandma.' Sophie reached for her jewellery box and lifted out the tray. Underneath was her diary. She drew out the photograph that was slipped inside it, and handed it to Katy. It had been taken on a snowy hillside and showed a man wearing a big black coat and a woolly hat. It was hard to make out his face but Sophie had spent so long studying his warm brown eyes and his big smile that she felt she could have known him anywhere.

'It's the only photo I've got of my dad,' she said.

'Oh, Sophie,' Katy said, putting an arm round her as she studied the photo.

'Mum threw all the rest away. I just managed to fish this one out before the bin men came.' She gazed at the photo. 'I used to be so angry with him when I looked at his picture. I almost tore it up myself, a couple of times.' She smiled. 'But now I know why he left ... to protect us.'

'He looks really nice,' Katy said. 'But I wouldn't keep the photo in your diary, if I were you. I'd put it somewhere safe.'

'Why?' Sophie said in surprise.

Katy wriggled uncomfortably. 'Well ... if I suspected someone was a witch, then their diary is one of the first places I'd look for clues.'

Sophie stared at her. 'Thanks, Katy,' she said, taking the photo. 'I never even thought of that!' She shivered at the thought of a witch hunter reading her diary. She wondered if Katy had ever found a witch by reading their diary before. But Sophie couldn't blame Katy for things she'd done in the past, before they were friends, before she knew that witches could be good.

Gally was running back and forth across the floor, as if he were looking for something. The boards squeaked and creaked.

'Sounds like a loose floorboard. The perfect hiding

place!' Sophie jumped up and pulled the rug to one side. 'Thanks, Gally.' She slipped her finger under the board and levered it up. Underneath was a dusty space. She put the photo in, dropped the floorboard down again and pulled the rug back over it.

'It'll be safe there,' she said. She couldn't help feeling worried, though. There was only one person at Turlingham who might search her room.

'You know . . . ' Sophie started. 'Ashton was trying to find things out about my family,' she told Katy. 'Then he recited the entire Gibson family tree off by heart! Was he just making it up?'

Katy shook her head. 'Not at all! Witch hunters are really proud of their lineages. I know it off by heart, too.'

'Seriously?' Sophie glanced at the computer. 'Can I test you?'

'Sure!' Katy grinned. 'I've not done this for ages.'

Sophie opened the website for the National Registry office, and they found the census records for Katy's family.

'OK – don't look.' Katy put her hands over her eyes.

'Right, now name your ... great-great-aunts on your mother's side!'

'Claudia, Phyllis, Jemima and Maud,' Katy said. 'Married to Paul Stokes, Joshua Whelts, Caloden Reace and Willard Michaels, respectively.'

'Whoa,' said Sophie.

Sophie tested her on generation after generation. Katy reeled off names without a single mistake.

'You're amazing!' Sophie said, shaking her head. 'OK, how about naming your mother's cousins' children ... your second cousins.'

'Easy!' Katy rattled off a list of names, finishing with, 'And the Lloyds, Heather and Miranda.'

'And ... ?' said Sophie. There was one more child listed: Robert Lloyd.

Katy shook her head. 'That's it.'

'Well, I'm glad you finally made a mistake! You were starting to freak me out,' Sophie laughed.

Katy took her hands from her eyes, creasing her forehead in confusion. 'I didn't make a mistake. I'm sure.'

'It's right here.' Sophie pointed. 'Robert Lloyd.'

Katy leaned forward and peered at the screen. 'I've never heard of him,' she said.

Sophie frowned.

'This is so interesting!' Katy's eyes lit up. 'Wow, a person in my family that I don't know about! That's incredible.'

Sophie half-laughed, half-sighed. 'I wish there was only *one* person I didn't know about in my family!'

Katy glanced at her sympathetically. 'You know, Sophie, we could use the internet to look up your father's family – the Poulters,' she suggested.

'Of course!' Sophie smiled, and turned back to the computer.

Katy stepped forward and clicked a few keys. 'Your grandma's name is Loveday, isn't it? Loveday Poulter. Not a common name ...'

'Oh, look! That's her!' Sophie pointed at the screen. 'Wow, born in 1940.'

Katy tapped the keys.

Sophie squealed as her father's information popped up. 'And there's my dad! Date of birth, 16th September, 1976. Place of birth, Durham. Name of father: Conrad

Poulter. Name of mother: Loveday Poulter, born Fairfield. Father's occupation: artist. Cool ... I wonder what he painted?'

'There's another Poulter here,' Katy said, leaning forward and clicking on the icon. 'Maybe it's a relation.'

The record came up. Sophie stared at the name: Gertrude Poulter. Her eyes moved to the date of birth: 16th September, 1976. Same as her father's.

'That's such a weird coincidence,' she began ... and tailed off as her eyes skimmed the rest of the information. The place of birth was Durham. The parents were Loveday and Conrad Poulter.

Katy broke the silence. 'Your father had a twin sister!'

Sophie shook her head, dumbstruck. Why had Grandma never mentioned her daughter? Why did no one tell her she had an aunt?

FIVE

Sophie dialled her grandma's number while Katy and Gally perched on the edge of the bed, watching her.

She waited as the phone rang and rang. She felt her hands start to sweat. How would she ask her about an aunt she'd never been told of? What if Aunt Gertrude was dead? Sophie would have to broach the subject carefully.

There was a click and her grandmother's voice said: 'Hello? Loveday Poulter here.'

'Grandma!' Sophie exclaimed. 'Why didn't you tell me about Gertrude?'

There was silence at the other end of the line. Sophie had forgotten to be careful, and she could have kicked herself for being so insensitive.

'Gertrude?' her grandma said finally. She sounded breathless. 'Er ... I don't know what you mean.'

'Grandma, I've seen a record of her birth,' Sophie said, feeling shocked. How could her grandmother deny that she had a child? She couldn't imagine her own mother ever pretending *she* didn't exist.

For a moment all she could hear were the beeps and far away voices of the machines and people in the hospital and Sophie thought her grandma wasn't going to reply. Then her sigh echoed down the line. 'Very well. It's true.' She sighed again. 'I *do* have a daughter, your father's twin sister. Gertrude.'

'But why don't you ever talk about her?'

'I can't explain now. Not on the phone.' There was the sound of a wheely trolley rolling in the hallway in the distance. 'Come and see me on Sunday. I'll tell you then.'

Sophie looked at Katy, sitting at the end of the bed. It suddenly struck her that this would be a great way to show Grandma that not all witch hunters were bad.

'I'll come,' she said, 'and I would like to bring my friend Katy as well.'

She heard her grandmother's sharp intake of breath. 'The witch hunter!'

'Grandma, she's my best friend!'

'Maybe you think so, but it was witch hunters who took my magic away from me.' Grandmother's voice trembled. 'You can't trust any of them.'

'Not all witch hunters are bad, Grandma. Katy lied to save me from her own parents, even though she knew I was a witch.'

Katy blushed. Sophie went on, smiling at her friend: 'I'd trust her with my life.'

'Sophie ...'

'Please, Grandma. It means a lot to me.'

There was a long pause, and Sophie held her breath. Finally her grandmother said: 'Very well. I'll see you both on Sunday.'

Sophie smiled in relief and gave Katy a thumbs up.

'Brilliant! We'll see you then. Oh, and Gran—' she added, as she suddenly remembered the other exciting thing that had happened that day, 'I found the strangest book in the school library!' She described *Magic Most Dark*: the metal clasps shaped like grinning faces, the rambling writing, the strange mixture of witch and witch-hunter writing. 'Where do you think it came from? Have you ever heard of anything like it before?'

'The nurses are calling me for dinner,' her grandmother replied quickly.

But Sophie hadn't heard anything.

'I have to go,' her grandmother said, sounding rattled. 'Good night!'

There was a click and a buzz – and Sophie found herself listening to the hum of a dead line.

'Just wait till you see it!' Sophie turned round to say to Katy as they hurried up the school stairs the next morning, their shoes echoing on the stone steps.

'Look out!' Katy shouted in reply. Sophie swung round just in time to stop herself bumping into Oliver at the top of the stairs.

'Whoops, sorry!' Sophie gasped.

'No problem,' he grinned. 'Hey, where are you off to?'

'The library,' Sophie said without thinking.

'Yeah, to, er, work on our History project,' Katy continued, slipping a warning arm through Sophie's.

Oliver's jaw dropped. 'You're not turning into Maggie Millar, are you? It's Saturday!'

'Yeah, but—' Sophie was about to make something up when Oliver interrupted.

'Are you going to see any of the others later? Like, um, Erin, or – or Kaz?' He raised his voice as Katy pulled Sophie away. 'We could all get together tonight, what do you think?'

'Yeah – maybe ...' Sophie waved and hurried off with Katy. She had magic on her mind!

The library was hushed and still, with sunbeams cutting down through the windows between the long rows of bookshelves and gleaming on the carvings in the wood. Sophie led the way towards the Rare Volumes Room. Inside it was as silent, dusty and deserted as ever.

'It's right here!' Sophie ran across to the radiator and peered down behind it.

But all she saw was cobwebs.

'Oh no!' she sobbed. 'It's gone!'

'Are you sure?' Katy came to join her. She stuck her hand down behind the radiator. 'Wait – I've got something.'

Katy pulled a piece of paper from behind the radiator and blew the dust from it. It was covered with random scribbles and lines, like a half-finished drawing. But as Katy turned it round and round, trying to make sense of them, a small symbol in the corner caught Sophie's eye.

'Look!'

'What?'

'That symbol's almost like the pattern that was on the air vent Kaz tripped over in the woods!' she cried.

Katy leaned in and looked closer. 'Oh yeah . . . Only the lines don't interweave in the same way – they're just vertical.' Katy frowned.

'How weird,' Sophie said, wondering what it could mean. 'Maybe it's something to do with the ventilation system in the school,' Sophie said. 'It's not the book, anyway – we might as well throw it away.'

'Let's keep it,' Katy said, folding it up and putting it in her pocket. 'You never know, it might be important.'

Sophie stared at the radiator. A horrible thought came into her head. 'Oh no ... I wonder if Ashton really did see the book and was just pretending not to?' She turned to Katy. 'Maybe he came back afterwards to steal it!'

Katy laughed and shook her head. 'No way. He wouldn't keep it quiet – he'd have to tell you so he could gloat!'

'I hope you're right,' sighed Sophie. But inside, she wasn't convinced. If Ashton hadn't taken it – who had? And were witches safe if the thief could use the spell to hunt them down?

Evening light shone through the school windows as Sophie and her friends tiptoed along the corridors towards the boys' dormitories. Sophie hadn't forgotten about the book, but she had another mission to see through – Operation: Get Erin and Mark to Kiss!

She realised she was alone, and turned round to see where her friends had got to. They were huddled by a classroom door, whispering loudly.

'Shhh, guys!' she hissed back at them. 'We don't want Mr Wilkinson to hear us!'

Joanna looked back at her and beckoned. Sophie hurried back on tiptoe. She found Erin in the centre of the huddle, teary with nerves.

'I don't think I can do this,' Erin whispered, looking panic stricken. 'It'll be so embarrassing – what if he doesn't want to kiss me?'

'Of course he does!' Kaz burst out, but Sophie shushed her. She could see that Erin was really upset.

'You know what?' she said. 'We need some magic to help you relax – like we did in the lighthouse a few weeks ago, do you remember?'

'Yeah, even though it's just a game, it'll help you calm down,' Katy said at once. 'Great idea, Soph.'

She pushed open the door to the classroom. They tiptoed in and sat in a circle. Sophie went to the window and looked out. She needed something to make her spell work as well as possible – and she found the perfect thing: a sweet-smelling jasmine bush growing in the moonlight. She plucked a sprig and turned back.

'Jasmine has got calming effects,' she told the others. It was true, but the spell would magnify those effects until they were very powerful. That was her secret idea, anyway. She had never tried to enchant an object before. She hoped it would work!

She took off her gold earrings with the daisies on them and rubbed the jasmine all over them. As she did so, she began to chant, using the words that came to her naturally.

'Earth, water, wind and fire . . . Forces of the Earth. Give us your strength . . . '

Jo giggled and Lauren joined in. Sophie smiled as she felt the tingle of magic surge through her, leaving her strong and calm and powerful. The smell of jasmine filled the room, and the earring shone an even deeper gold.

Sophie stopped chanting as she sensed the spell was complete, and held her earrings out to Erin.

'You're letting me borrow them?' Erin exclaimed. 'But they're your faves!'

'They'll bring you good luck,' said Sophie. 'And I want them back,' she added with a smile.

Erin clipped them on, and a puzzled but pleased look came over her face.

'Actually ... I really do feel calmer! How weird is that?' She got to her feet. 'OK, girls, ready if you are!'

Sophie and Katy exchanged delighted grins – it looked as if the spell had worked!

Sophie could hear muffled voices as they approached the boys' dorm.

'They're definitely not asleep!' Kaz whispered. Light shone under the door and Sophie could even hear music being played through headphones. She peered through the crack of the door, beckoning the others over. Oliver was sprawled in a chair by the window, flicking through a football magazine. Mark was sitting on a bed in his pyjamas, gelling his hair. Sophie stifled a giggle. Their dorm was a mess compared to the girls' – socks and shirts strewn everywhere.

'You *do* fancy her, Ollie,' Mark was saying. 'It's obvious!'

'Not really!' Oliver protested, but he was blushing as he pretended to read the magazine. Sophie shared a look with Katy: *who was the 'her'?*

Sophie leaned in – and froze as the door creaked loudly.

'What was that?' Mark jumped up from the bed and headed towards the door. Sophie shooed the others in front of her, and they fled, screeching, down the corridor. Erin dived into the common room and the girls followed her. Jo and Lauren ducked behind the pile of beanbags, and Kaz hid under the pool table. Sophie and Katy hid in the shadows near the book cases, and Erin went into the games cupboard.

After several minutes, Erin poked her head out.

'Isn't he coming?' She sounded disappointed.

'I know!' Sophie whispered. 'Send Mark a text telling him there's a surprise for him inside the cupboard!' The door to the bathroom was open. 'We'll hide in the boys' bathroom. Then you'll have him all to yourself!'

Erin looked nervous but excited.

'OK!' she whispered, and ducked back, her phone already in her hand.

Sophie herded her friends into the bathroom, and they pulled the door shut almost completely, leaving just a crack so they could still peer out.

'Now, shhh!' Sophie whispered to them.

The giggling and the whispering died down, and she watched through the crack of the door.

A beam of light sprang into the room, and Sophie heard the sound of voices and footsteps coming down the corridor towards them.

'Oh no,' Kaz whispered behind her. 'He's brought his friends!'

Sophie's heart sank. Erin and Mark would never get to kiss with all the boys there!

The door of the common room was pushed open and Mark went over to the cupboard. With his friends crowded round, he opened the door.

'Surprise!' Sophie heard Erin call out with a giggle.

'Erin!' Mark sounded shocked but delighted.

The boys roared with laughter. The next moment

they were shoving Mark into the cupboard with Erin. Oliver put his back against the door and the others joined him, pushing it shut. The door resounded with thumps, and then suddenly the thumping stopped. The boys snorted with laughter. Sophie counted slowly to twenty then burst out of the bathroom with the others following. The boys spun round, startled, then started laughing again as the girls barged through them.

'Enough's enough!' said Lauren. 'Time to uncage the lovebirds.'

Sophie pulled the door open. Erin and Mark tumbled out, blushing but looking pleased.

'So, did you like your surprise?' Kaz asked.

'Yeah, thanks, girls!' Mark grinned and put his arm round Erin.

'What were you doing in there, eh? Eh?' Lauren stood on tiptoe to peer over Katy's shoulder.

'Mind your own!' Erin grinned.

Sophie checked her watch and saw it was time for her to go – her mother had said she had to be back by nine. 'See you later, guys.'

Erin stepped forward. 'Thanks, Soph – the good-luck charm worked!' she said with a wink.

'Good!' Sophie smiled. 'You'll have to tell me all about it later.'

As Sophie walked down the corridor, she heard running feet behind her.

'Sophie!' It was Kaz. 'Listen – I just wanted to ask you a favour.'

'Of course!' said Sophie, surprised.

Kaz swallowed a few times before blurting out: 'C-could you find out what Callum thinks of me? You know, if he'd ever maybe want to go on a date with me?' She added, 'I just, you know – I've got to know how he feels! Please, Soph.'

Sophie swallowed her amazement. She'd never seen Kaz nervous before. It looked as if she was seriously into Callum ... but he liked Katy.

'Um ...' Sophie mumbled. *Maybe I should warn her*, she thought. She didn't want Kaz to get hurt. But on the other hand, he hadn't actually asked Katy out yet, so ...

Kaz didn't wait for a reply. 'Just tell me as soon as

you know anything, OK?' she said, with a lopsided smile. 'Thanks, Sophie!'

'You're welcome,' Sophie said faintly as Kaz ran off back down the corridor. She pushed back her hair and sighed. *How am I going to handle this one?*

SIX

Sophie led Katy up the sweeping drive that led from the main road to the Bowden Psychiatric Hospital. As they stepped inside, the receptionist looked up and smiled a welcome.

'Hi, Sumira – we've come to see Grandma,' Sophie said.

'Yes, your mum phoned to say you were on your way. Go on through!'

Sophie led Katy along the sunny corridors towards Grandma's room.

'That's the day room, and that's where they have their meals,' she pointed out as they went past. 'Oh, and they've got the new paintings up! They do all these brilliant art activities here.' She turned down Grandma's corridor.

Behind her, Katy cleared her throat anxiously. 'Is she . . . is she nice, Sophie? Your granny, I mean?'

'Of course she's nice!' Sophie laughed. 'You're not worried, are you?'

'Just a bit.' Katy bit her lip then said, 'I mean, she hates witch hunters, doesn't she?'

Sophie stopped and gave Katy a big smile. She was feeling a little anxious about them meeting but she didn't want to worry Katy. 'She'll like you as soon as she sees you,' she said. 'Come on.'

She stopped at the white door marked with her grandmother's name. It was normally left open, but not today, so Sophie knocked and they stood in silence, waiting . . .

'Maybe she's fallen asleep,' Sophie said with a frown.

She pushed the door open and called into the room: 'Grandma? It's Sophie!'

There was no answer, so Sophie went in. She saw at a glance that the room was empty. The bathroom door was ajar, and Grandma's dressing gown lay on the floor. The window was open.

'Grandma,' Sophie called, bending to pick up the dressing gown. She placed it on the bed as Katy tapped on the bathroom door, then pushed it fully open.

'No one there,' Katy reported. 'Could she have gone somewhere?'

'I suppose she might be in the day room,' Sophie agreed. She led Katy back down the corridor. But there were only three people in there, watching television, and none of them were her grandma.

'I'll check the gardens – she sometimes goes out there,' Sophie said. A sudden feeling of nervousness shot through her. *There's no need to worry*, she told herself. 'Katy, will you go back and ask Sumira if she's seen her?'

'Of course,' Katy nodded. She headed towards the reception, and Sophie went out into the gardens.

Sophie searched the gardens and the hospital corridors, but there was no sign of Grandma. She ran back to Grandma's room – and found Katy and Sumira hurrying towards her.

'You didn't find her?' Sumira called as Sophie approached. She looked worried. Sophie's heart beat fast as she shook her head. 'I'll call security and we'll have a good look round. Don't worry, Sophie. I'm sure she's fine.' Sumira turned and raced back to the reception desk.

'Let's go and wait in reception,' said Katy, putting an arm round Sophie's shoulders.

As they reached reception Sophie saw a security guard run past, his radio crackling. Nurses hurried here and there, opening doors and checking inside. Sophie watched them, her chest feeling tight. What if Grandma had collapsed somewhere? What if she was really ill? What if the witch hunters ...

She felt a hand on her shoulder and looked up into Sumira's worried face.

'Sophie, love, we can't find her. We're going to call your mother.'

Sophie and Katy were still in the reception twenty minutes later when the hospital doors slid open and her mother came through at a run, followed by a policeman.

'Mum!' Sophie jumped up and ran to her.

'Darling!' Her mother hugged her, saying: 'I have to go and talk to the warden. You stay here with Katy and wait for me, OK?'

Her mother disappeared through the door of the warden's office. Sophie went back to sit with Katy.

'Oh, Sophie, try not to worry. I'm sure she'll turn up safe and sound,' Katy said, squeezing Sophie's hand.

Sophie nodded and forced a smile as she squeezed back. She searched her memory, trying to think where Grandma might have gone to. She'd *told* them to come on Sunday, she had been expecting them. Although she had acted oddly on the phone. Especially when Sophie had asked her about *Magic Most Dark*. In fact ... that had been the last thing they had spoken about, hadn't it? Sophie heaved a worried sigh.

Through the warden's door, Sophie heard the voices rising and falling. The warden's voice became louder and she made out the words '... never happened before ... she's one of our most trusted patients ...'

Sophie and Katy exchanged a glance.

'Oh, Sophie,' Katy said, her voice shaking, 'what if she ran away because of me? What if she was afraid of me because ... ' She didn't say it but the words *I'm a witch hunter* hung in the air.

Sophie shook her head with more confidence than she felt. 'Of course not! I'm sure there'll be some completely ordinary explanation.'

'I hope you're right,' Katy sighed. 'I would never forgive myself if it was my fault.'

'It's not!' Sophie said. *But it might be mine*, she thought. She felt sick as she remembered her slip of the tongue when she'd been talking to Ashton. She'd let him know that her father had a female relative. What if he had found out about Grandma? What if the Gibsons had somehow captured her?

There was no way she would make Katy feel bad by suggesting that aloud. She would just have to worry about it alone.

She concentrated on the voices behind the door.

A deep male voice – the policeman, she guessed – was saying, 'We'll go and have a look at her room and see if we can find anything there, if that's all right with you.'

Sophie jumped to her feet with a gasp. Katy looked up at her, startled.

'Come on!' Sophie whispered, pulling her to her feet. 'We've got to search Grandma's room before the police do!'

They sprinted down the corridors, Sophie in the lead. She burst in through the door of her grandmother's room. A glance round showed her what she hadn't thought to notice before: her grandmother had left in a hurry. The window was open and so were the drawers. Her handbag was missing from its usual peg and her coat was gone, too. Sophie relaxed a little. If Grandma had taken her coat and bag, she probably hadn't been kidnapped, at least.

Something under the bed rustled and scuttled.

'What was that?' Katy looked startled.

'I don't know!' Sophie dropped down on her hands and knees and peered under the bed. It seemed as if a patch of darkness was moving. Then she spotted a yellow eye and realised the rustling was feathers.

'Corvis!' she shrieked as the raven flapped out from under the bed and flew to the lampshade. It perched, there, swinging. There was an envelope in its beak.

'It's Grandma's familiar,' Sophie told Katy, breathlessly. 'Corvis, give me that envelope!'

The bird launched itself from the lampshade and sailed towards the window. Katy blocked it just in time, and the bird circled round, landing on the chest of drawers. Sophie was just wondering how to catch it when Gally jumped out of her pocket and leapt after him. The squirrel skidded across the chest of drawers and bumped into the raven, and with a startled *Caaark!* from Corvis they tumbled off and fell down the back of the sofa. Sophie clapped her hands to her mouth, hoping they weren't hurt, and scrambled onto the sofa to look down. Gally shot out from under the sofa, clutching the envelope. Corvis hopped after him, shaking out his feathers.

'Thanks, Gally!' Sophie took the envelope from him. 'I'm sorry, Corvis. I know you're trying to protect Grandma's things but we're really worried about her.'

Corvis stayed perched on the back of the sofa, looking on as Sophie opened the envelope. Her heart was beating fast. She had hoped it would be a letter from Grandma, explaining her disappearance – but it wasn't.

'A postcard of Durham cathedral?' she said blankly.

'Let me see,' Katy came over and together they read the words on the back of the postcard.

It's happened.

F

'What on earth does that mean?' Sophie said.

Katy shook her head, looking as puzzled as Sophie felt.

Sophie looked into the envelope again.

'Oh look – there's something else!' she exclaimed as she pulled out a folded piece of paper. As she unfolded it, both she and Katy gasped. It was almost exactly like the piece of paper they had found behind the radiator yesterday, in the place where the magic book had been.

'Look – it's got the same kind of half-finished

drawing on it,' Katy pointed out. 'And the square symbol in the corner – except *these* lines go in the opposite direction!'

'This is my Grandma's handwriting!' Sophie pointed to a name and a list of numbers scrawled across the bottom of the paper.

'Chris Seaply,' Katy read. 'And I guess this must be Chris Seaply's phone number.'

100 130 4298

'So . . . we should call him—'

'Or her.'

'Yeah, and see if they know anything about your grandmother!' Katy said.

Sophie nodded. She knew it was a long shot. The phone number could be nothing to do with Grandma's disappearance – but it was worth a try.

Corvis gave a sudden, warning caw, and flew out of the window.

Sophie could hear footsteps tramping towards them, so she hastily stuffed the paper into her pocket.

'What are you kids doing in here?' the policeman asked gruffly as he pushed open the door.

'Um ... we were just double-checking Grandma wasn't here,' Sophie said, hoping he wouldn't get suspicious.

The policeman's face softened. 'Why don't you let us take a look? Off you go now – back to your mum.'

Sophie and Katy scurried out into the corridor. Sophie hoped she had done the right thing, hiding the note from the police. There was so much she wished she'd had time to talk to Grandma about. Like the magic book ...

Of course! she thought. *The book!* She remembered the spell she'd glimpsed in it: *To Find Any Named Witch*. If they could find the book again, they could use that spell to find Grandma!

SEVEN

Sophie pushed open the door to the common room and she and Katy walked in.

'You're back!' Erin jumped up from the desk where she had been working and ran over to greet them. Joanna and Lauren left their beanbags, and Kaz unplugged her iPod and joined them.

'Oh, Sophie, I got your text about your grandma,' Lauren said, her eyes full of sympathy.

'Yeah, we're so sorry.' Kaz put an arm round Sophie's shoulders. 'But I'm sure she'll be found safe and sound.'

'Totally,' Erin agreed, and the others nodded.

Sophie found herself blinking back tears as her friends hugged her.

'Thanks so much, guys,' she said, putting her bag down. 'I'm supposed to wait here until Mum gets back.'

'Is she looking for her now?' Kaz asked.

Sophie nodded. 'I wanted to stay but she wouldn't let me. She said I should just wait in the common room and try and concentrate on my homework.'

'Well, we're all doing our family tree projects,' said Kaz. 'I discovered that no one in my family has ever done anything interesting at all! I'm so amazed – not.'

Sophie laughed. She felt so lucky that she had friends who could make her smile, even at the worst times.

'I found that my great-grandfather was one of the world's first professional football players!' said Jo, sounding surprised but pleased. 'How about you, Sophie? Did you find out anything interesting about your family?'

Sophie and Katy exchanged a guilty look.

'Nah, they're all boring,' Sophie said, crossing her fingers behind her back. 'But you're right – we ought to get on with it.'

She pulled out a chair and sat down. Katy took the seat next to her. Sophie whispered to her. 'Let's do this really quickly, then we can try to phone that number.'

Katy nodded. Sophie pulled out her papers and started working. It was easy, because she was just making up names – the hardest part was making it look as if she was doing proper research. After half an hour she nudged Katy. Katy nodded back and began collecting her papers.

'Wow, are you two done? That was quick!' Erin looked up, open-mouthed, as they stood up.

'I wish! We're just going to the library to look something up,' said Sophie as she headed to the door. 'See you!'

They walked down the corridor to the phone booth.

'Wow, this thing is like a museum relic!' Katy said, pulling open the creaky wooden door.

'I just hope it hasn't been disconnected.'

Sophie went in, and Katy squashed in too, joining her on the padded velvet seat. She picked up the heavy handset and dialled the number. A voice spoke at once. Sophie gave Katy the thumbs up, then realised it was a recording.

'This number is not in service. Please replace the handset and try again.'

'What happened?' Katy asked.

Sophie passed her the receiver. Katy frowned as she listened. 'Maybe we got it wrong. Let's try again.'

Sophie dialled the number once more, double-checking the digits. But they got the same message. She put the receiver down with a frustrated sigh.

'I know,' she said, noticing a peeling sticker on the glass panel in the door that read *118 Directory Enquiries.*

A few minutes later, Sophie had the numbers for three Chris Seapleys. It felt a bit weird to be ringing up complete strangers. But if they knew anything about her grandma, it would be worth it.

'Seapley residence, good afternoon,' said a woman's voice in her ear.

Sophie gulped. 'Oh, er, hello ... could I speak to Chris, please?'

'My name, young lady, is Mrs Christine Seapley. And who might *you* be?'

'Um, my name's Sophie. I'm phoning about my grandmother, Mrs Poulter? Loveday Poulter?'

'I have no idea what you are talking about, I'm afraid.'

'You don't know her? You're sure?' Sophie clutched the receiver.

'Quite certain. And let me tell you, I am not amused by nuisance calls! Good day!'

'But—'

The receiver clicked down firmly.

'She hung up on me,' said Sophie.

'Wow, grump-y,' Katy huffed.

'Would you do the next one, please,' Sophie groaned, passing Katy the receiver.

But after two more phone calls, they found none of the Chris Seapleys knew anything about Sophie's grandmother.

'Now what?' said Sophie as they went out of the

phone booth. She bit her lip as she remembered the magic book she'd had in her hands for just a second. 'If only we could find *Magic Most Dark* again,' she said. 'I saw a spell in there for locating witches ...'

Her phone bleeped. It was a text from her mum.

I'm back at home. No news of Grandma. Come back, it's getting dark and I need a hug.

Sophie sighed and showed Katy the text. 'I'll see you tomorrow, OK? Maybe we'll think of a way to find her overnight.'

EIGHT

'Great projects, class. I can see you really enjoyed doing this,' Mr McGowan announced as he walked up and down the room, handing back the family trees.

'And Sophie . . . ' Mr McGowan paused by her desk, a broad smile on his face, 'you've turned out to have a truly fascinating family!'

Sophie frowned. 'I have?'

'Why, yes!' Mr McGowan turned to the class, beaming. 'Sophie has discovered that she is a relation of Lord Kinver of Kettleby Magna . . . who happens to be a cousin of the Turlingham family. That makes our Sophie distantly related to our very own Earl Marmaduke of Turlingham.'

There was a scrape of chairs as the others turned round to gape at her. Sophie blushed and sank down into her seat.

'As you probably know, the Sunday night after half term is the usual Pagan Parade in Turlingham village,' Mr McGowan went on. 'It's a celebration of old English culture, with floats and a procession. And since Sophie is related to the Turlingham family it seems only right that she should ride on the family float!'

Sophie sat bolt upright. 'Um – sorry?'

Mr McGowan beamed at her broadly. 'I know! Isn't it exciting? I've arranged it personally. Marmaduke is in my morris-dancing troupe, you see. He thought it was a wonderful idea.'

'I, I, er . . . ' Sophie began, but Mr McGowan had already moved on. Katy threw her a teeth-clenching glance of sympathy. Callum looked back over his shoulder, struggling not to laugh. Sophie made a face at him and dropped her head into her hands. The last thing she wanted was to be stuck on a float for the whole world to see – and besides, what if someone found out she'd been lying?

'Traditionally, it's a masked parade,' Mr McGowan was continuing, 'and I will take to the festival any student who makes a mask.'

'That's awesome!' exclaimed Erin. 'Almost as cool as a masked ball! I'll have to coordinate my costume with Mark.'

Sophie glanced round for inspiration, and saw the tip of Gally's black tail whisking out of her bag. She grinned. A squirrel costume would be perfect! She opened her mouth to say so, but Mr McGowan broke in: 'There'll be plenty of time to discuss that later, girls. For now, it's back to Henry VIII ...'

Once his back was turned, Sophie reached down and gave Gally a quick stroke as a thank you for the inspiration. Being on the float wouldn't be so embarrassing if no one could see who she was!

'What do you all think about another midnight feast tonight?' Kaz whispered. 'We haven't been into the old lighthouse for ages!'

'Good idea!' Sophie smiled. She needed something to stop her worrying about Grandma, she thought – and a midnight feast sounded perfect.

Sophie paused to get her breath as she reached the top of the lighthouse stairs, then pushed open the door to the lantern room. It was a clear, frosty night, and the moonlight shone in through the dusty glass windows. The huge lantern cast shadows over the room. It would almost have been spooky, Sophie thought, if she hadn't been able to hear Erin saying loudly, 'Jo, your mum's cookies get better and better, I swear!' and Kaz's iPod playing the Grease Monkeys' new single.

Sophie followed the noise around the lantern and found her friends sharing out the chocolates and cakes for the midnight feast.

'Sophie! You managed to sneak out!' Katy jumped up and made room for her on the blanket.

'Yes – though I felt kind of guilty because Mum's so worried.' Sophie sighed.

'So you didn't hear anything about your grand-mother yet?' Lauren asked.

Sophie shook her head and sat down. She wondered where her grandma was at that very moment. She hoped she had somewhere warm to sleep and wasn't wandering the streets . . .

'Come on, we're supposed to be taking my mind *off* my grandma,' she said, trying to smile. 'What are you all doing for half term?'

'I think we're going camping,' Kaz said, making a face. 'I don't know why Dad does it – last time the tent caught fire and he dropped his glasses down the Portaloo.'

The girls giggled.

'I'm going to stay with my Irish relatives in Dublin over half term,' Erin said. She sighed.

'Don't you like them?' Sophie said, feeling sorry for her. Erin's parents lived in America so she couldn't go home for half term.

'Oh no, they're really nice! But I'll have to spend a whole week away from—'

'Maaaark!' the others chorused, exchanging knowing glances. Erin laughed and covered her blushing face with her hands.

'I ... I think I love him!' she said through her fingers.

'Aw, that's so cute!' Kaz sighed. 'So tell us, what was it like kissing him?'

'Wonderful!'

'But what was it *like*?' Jo demanded.

'Yeah, we want the juicy details!' Sophie agreed.

'Oh, I don't know ... I can't describe it ... it was just amazing.' Erin took her hands from her face. 'But I know we're meant for each other now ... I'm so in love with him.'

'That's so sweet,' Katy said. She swallowed and added, 'Actually – I have a confession to make. I've got a crush too!'

The girls squealed.

'Really? Who?' Jo demanded.

Katy wriggled, blushing and grinning at the same time. 'It's – promise you won't tell him! – Callum.'

Sophie glanced quickly over at Kaz. She wasn't smiling.

'Oh, come on, is that supposed to be news?' Erin teased Katy.

'Yeah, we knew that, duh!' Lauren giggled.

'I didn't,' said Kaz, so quietly that only Sophie heard her. Sophie winced and opened her mouth to change the subject. But before she had a chance, Kaz went on defiantly: 'Callum's *my* crush, everyone knows that.'

'He is?' Katy's mouth fell open and she stared at Kaz.

'Yes!' Kaz said, folding her arms. 'I've liked him for ages, since before you came to the school.'

There was an uncomfortable silence.

'Hey, girlfriends!' Erin burst out. She put an arm round each girl's shoulders and pulled them towards her. 'Let's not get upset about it, OK?'

'Erin's right,' Sophie said. 'Callum's really nice but girlfriends are friends for ever – we can't let boys come between us!'

Kaz and Katy scowled at each other – then Katy forced a smile.

'I guess you're right,' she said. 'It's silly to argue about it – we don't even know how he feels about either of us.'

'Exactly!' Sophie said in relief. She put on a mock-stern face. 'Now I'm ordering you two to make a pinky promise not to break friends over it!'

Katy made a face and Kaz sighed.

'Come on! Make friends, make friends, never ever break friends . . .' Erin took Katy and Kaz's hands and put them together.

'Oh, all right,' Katy laughed. Kaz laughed too, and the two of them joined little fingers.

'Yay!' Erin and Sophie high-fived each other over their linked fingers. Katy and Kaz joined in the laughter.

'May the best girl win!' said Kaz. 'Now pass me those fig rolls.'

Sophie handed them over ... wishing she wasn't already certain that Callum thought Katy was the best girl!

Sophie bent over the keyboard of the library catalogue computer, Katy at her side.

Magic Most Dark, she typed, and hit return. She watched the screen as the results loaded ...

'Nothing!' she said in disappointment. She rested her chin on her hands, frowning in thought. They *had* to find the book – without it, she didn't know how they were going to find Grandma.

She looked up. Katy was staring across the library as if hypnotised. Sophie followed her gaze and sighed – Callum had just taken a seat at one of the other computers.

'I'll just go and say hello ...' Katy headed towards him. Sophie followed her. They would never find the book at this rate!

Callum looked up as Katy reached him. 'Oh, hi! Hi!' He jumped to his feet, almost knocking his chair over. 'Would you like my seat?'

'Oh ... no ... I just wondered what you were doing.'

'Playing Elfin Warriors. I'm on level thirty-two now!' Callum said proudly.

Sophie shook her head in despair. Callum looked at her as if he had only just noticed her.

'Oh ... hi, Sophie. What are you two up to?' he asked.

'Looking for a book,' Sophie told him. 'The title's not in the catalogue.'

Callum nodded seriously. 'Have you tried the reference number?' he asked. He glanced at their blank faces. 'You know all books have a special reference number? If you have the number you can look for it that way.' He turned over a Maths book lying next to him. 'Like this one, see?'

Sophie gasped at the long number Callum pointed at and grabbed Katy's arm, pulling her back to the computer.

'Uh – bye, Callum!' Katy tossed over her shoulder.

'That long number next to the name Chris Seapley – it could easily be a reference number, not a phone number!' Sophie sat down at the computer and began to type the number into the library catalogue. They stared at the screen while the computer hummed. Finally, the title flashed up.

'*Magic Most Dark*!' Katy's eyes were wide.

Sophie clapped her hands. 'So the number scribbled on the note we found in Grandma's room is the reference number for *Magic Most Dark*!'

'But how did your grandma find that out?'

Sophie shook her head. 'I don't know – but it says

it's in the library – on aisle one hundred and thirty-eight!'

'Let's go!' Katy said, squeezing Sophie's hand.

They set off into the library, counting down the aisles.

'... forty-seven, forty-eight, forty-nine ...' Katy trailed off as they reached the last set of bookshelves. 'There are only forty-nine aisles. Where's one hundred and thirty-eight?'

Sophie looked round her. They were next to the private study rooms. She glanced down the wall until she saw a small, familiar door – the Rare Volumes Room.

On impulse, she turned the handle and went in. The room was as cold and dusty as before. She could see at a glance that the bookcase was numbered fifty.

'There aren't any more bookshelves,' Sophie looked down at the piece of paper again. 'Something must be wrong.'

'Maybe we should try a search on the name Chris Seapley,' Katy suggested.

They raced back to the computer. Sophie sat down in the chair and typed in the name under the *find by author* bar. She hit return and they waited, Sophie chewing her nail anxiously. She sighed as the screen showed her no results.

'Where *is* this book?' she groaned.

'We can't have missed—' Katy said, then hurriedly straightened up and smoothed her hair as Callum headed towards them.

'Callum,' Sophie said on the spur of the moment, 'you've never heard of this author, have you?' She showed him the piece of paper.

'Chris Seapley?' Callum frowned at it. 'No, I haven't.' He chuckled. 'Hey . . . cool.'

'What?' Sophie looked at him hopefully.

'Oh, just that his name's an anagram for Real Physics.' Callum blushed. 'Er . . . that wasn't quite as funny as I thought, was it?'

Sophie ignored him. '*Real Physics* could be a title . . .!' she exclaimed.

Katy squealed. 'Callum, that's amazing!' She flung her arms round him, then jolted away, blushing.

Callum staggered, looking delighted and embarrassed.

Sophie left them stuttering apologies at each other and ran back to the computer. She typed Real Physics under the *find by title* bar.

'It's there!' she burst out as Katy reached her. 'On shelf fifty.'

'No way!' Katy grasped her arm. 'Come on – let's go.'

They raced back to the Rare Volumes Room. Sophie looked along the shelves, reading the titles of the books. She spotted a slim book bound in dark-red leather. The title was picked out in gold: *Real Physics*.

'Katy, I've found it!' she cried. 'Maybe *Magic Most Dark* is behind this one?' She pulled the book out. As soon as she did, there was a grating noise and a sudden cold draught swept around her.

'Um ... Sophie?' Katy's voice was full of fear and excitement.

Sophie turned. An arched doorway had appeared in the back wall of the room. She stared at it, speechless.

'The wall just slid open. It happened when you moved the book.' Katy's voice trembled.

Sophie moved forward, breathless with astonishment. With Katy at her side, she stepped through the secret door, glancing up nervously. It was made of large, ancient-looking blocks of grey stone, carved into a pointed arch, like a church window. Beyond the door, spiral stairs disappeared into shadows.

'I wonder where it leads?' Katy murmured.

Sophie swallowed. 'There's only one way to find out,' she said. 'Come on!'

NINE

Sophie made her way down the stairs slowly. Katy was so close behind her that she could hear her nervous breathing. On the walls, lit candles in sconces wavered in the draught.

There was a sudden sigh of wind, the candle flames bowed, and the passage became much darker. Sophie spun round. The door had closed itself behind them, and a metallic grinding sound told her that the door was now locked. Getting out might not be as easy as getting in!

The stairs led them down and round, down and round.

'They go on for ever!' Katy whispered.

'Maybe we're heading underground,' Sophie whispered back.

Finally they reached the bottom of the stairs. To one side was a long stone wall, disappearing into shadows. To the other, shadowy rows of bookshelves stretched away. More candles cast a flickering light.

'It's so quiet,' Katy whispered. 'And cold! It feels as if no one's been here for centuries!'

'I can't believe all this is hidden inside the school!' Sophie murmured, glancing along the seemingly endless aisles. 'I wonder if the teachers know? I wonder if *my mum* knows?'

Katy shook her head. 'I'm sure this place is magic. Your mum can't possibly know.'

Sophie knew Katy was right. She could feel magic all around her, like the moisture in the air. Turlingham was old – but did it also have a connection to witchcraft? Was that possible?

Distantly, she heard a voice, coming and going as if it were being blown by the breeze.

'*Romeo, Romeo . . .*'

Sophie listened hard. It couldn't possibly be . . .

'Katy,' she said, 'I know this sounds mad, but can you hear . . . Erin?'

Katy cocked her head on one side and listened. 'Yes!' she exclaimed.

'It's coming from this direction,' Sophie said, puzzled. She followed the sound along the wall and saw an air vent in the ceiling – exactly like the one that Kaz had tripped over in the forest. Erin's voice was echoing down it faintly.

'*. . . deny thy father and, um, what was it? Oh yeah, refuse thy name . . .*'

Sophie couldn't help but laugh, and Katy did too.

'I bet that vent leads to the Drama studio,' said Sophie. 'Erin and the others went to rehearse for *Romeo and Juliet.*'

'Wow!' Katy stared up the shadowy vent. 'No wonder it's always freezing in there!'

Sophie grinned. It was fun to think that they were underneath the school, secretly, without anyone knowing. Then she remembered that they had a serious job to do.

Turning round, she glimpsed a small metal plate attached to the closest bookshelf.

'Look – the aisles are numbered!' she said in relief. 'This one's fifty-one.' She glanced at Katy. 'We should find aisle one hundred and thirty-eight pretty quickly.'

Sophie led the way along the aisle, gazing round her, wide-eyed. The shelves were packed with old books. Candlelight glinted from gold lettering on the spines. She looked up and spotted carvings of animals running along the top of the bookshelves, just like the ones in the library above. But instead of squirrels and birds and butterflies, the carvings were of bats and owls and moths ... night-time animals. She pointed them out to Katy, who shivered.

'It's like the underworld of the library!' she whispered to Sophie, glancing into the shadows.

'Katy, why are we whispering?'

'I don't know – it just feels as if we should!'

They giggled.

'I wonder how Grandma's connected to *Magic Most*

Dark . . . ' Sophie tailed off as she saw that the next bookshelf stood against a wall, blocking their way. She peered down the bookshelf. Beyond it, she could see more aisles, the candles flickering away into the gloom.

'This is aisle one hundred and thirty,' Katy read from the end of the bookshelf. 'Aisle one hundred and thirty-eight must be that way.' She pointed.

'Come on – we're nearly there!' Sophie broke into a run. When they got to the end of the row of book-shelves she turned right and counted up eight more, then looked for the number.

'Katy!' she said excitedly. 'This one says eighty-four!'

'What? But it can't be!' Katy read the number and frowned. 'What about the one next to it?'

'That's two hundred and twenty-nine,' Sophie reported after a moment. 'But I don't understand . . .'

'Wait – I'll go and look.' Katy raced off along the corridor that ran along the ends of the rows, looking at the shelf numbers. She came back shaking her head. 'There's no order to them!' she said. 'It's completely illogical.'

'So weird,' Sophie said with a frown. 'Well, I guess we just have to keep looking until we stumble across aisle 138.'

Katy shrugged and looked round. 'This way?' she suggested, waving at the closest aisle.

'I suppose! What else can we do?' Sophie agreed.

As they walked, Sophie glanced at the titles of the books and read them out.

'*Mysterious Mushrooms*,' she said. 'That one sounds weird!'

'Or what about this – *The Unexpected Unicorn*!' Katy laughed.

'Oh and look – this one's beautiful,' Sophie said, stopping at a huge book with a glittering beehive decorating the spine. '*Bee-Keeping for the 16th-Century Gentleman*.'

She lifted it off the shelf and began turning the heavy, silky pages. The script looked like little bees climbing all over the page to form the letters. Katy craned over her shoulder. 'Wow, look at the detail – it's as if you could reach out and touch it.' Sophie turned the page. 'Oh—'

In the illustration, a man was fleeing out of the picture, a look of terror on his face. A golden cloud of bees was flying after him. Sophie giggled, but stopped as she felt, and then heard, a deep humming sound. It vibrated through the book and made her hands tingle.

Suddenly feeling uncomfortable, she closed the book and put it back on the shelf. The buzzing sound still hummed in her ears.

'Can you hear that?' she asked Katy.

Katy nodded.

'It's like . . . '

As she spoke, a glittering cloud swept round the corner of the aisle. Sophie stared. *Bees!*

'Run!' she shouted, heading away from the swarm. Katy followed her. They ducked into the next row of bookshelves, but one glance behind told Sophie that the bees were still coming. She raced up that aisle and dodged into the next, trying to shake them off.

'We're lost!' Katy panted as they raced past aisle number 890. She shrieked as a bee got into her hair.

'Just keep going!' Sophie gasped.

As they came to the end of the aisle, Sophie saw that

they had reached the long wall again. In the ceiling she saw the air vent that led to the Drama studio.

'Look!' she pointed to it. 'The exit's got to be nearby.' She ran along the wall and Katy followed her. Finally, she found the stairs and raced up them, gasping for breath.

Katy overtook her, and came to a breathless halt.

'The door's shut!' She hammered on it.

Sophie looked back down the spiral stairs. The noise of the bees was getting louder – and they sounded furious. She grabbed a candle from one of the wall sconces. 'Heat! We need more heat,' she cried. She bent down and set the candle on the steps below her.

'Earth, water, air and fire, defend us!' she chanted, and gestured as if she was pulling the candle flame up and around them in a shield. There was a surge of heat as the flame grew, and suddenly there was a golden wall of flickering fire between them and the bees.

Sophie backed away, shielding her face from the heat.

Katy was feeling the door. 'There's no handle . . . just these two metal plates, one on each side.'

Sophie glanced at the plates. They had a geometric design, one with horizontal lines, the other with vertical ones.

'Push them together,' she said urgently. 'They might make some kind of lock, or handle ...' She pressed the left-hand one, and Katy copied her, pushing the right-hand one inwards.

The plate moved suddenly and smoothly under her hand, and the two plates locked into each other with a *click-clunk*, the lines weaving together. The wall grated open, and they ran out into the Rare Volumes Room. She flinched as a bee buzzed past, and glanced back. The wall of flames was dying down. Some of the bees were getting through. 'How do we shut it?' Katy shrieked again, flapping as a bee circled her.

Sophie glimpsed *Real Physics* lying on its side where she had left it. She grabbed it and slotted it back in its place. The doorway slid closed, and the noise of the crackling flames and buzzing bees disappeared.

Sophie leaned against the bookshelf, panting. A stray bee buzzed and bumped at the window.

'This is dangerous stuff,' she said, as soon as she had

her breath back. 'We could have got lost, or stung to death, or anything. But I've got to get that book – it's the only way I can think of to find my grandma.'

Katy nodded. 'You're right. Only when can we explore the library without anyone finding out? It'd have to be when no one's around ...' She caught Sophie's eye.

'Half term!' they chorused together.

'Perfect timing,' grinned Sophie. 'We'll just have to persuade your parents to let you stay at mine for the week!'

Sophie had to hope that a week would give them time to find the book, and then find Grandma.

TEN

Sophie leaned the get-well card she'd made for Erin against the back of the bus seat and carefully drew another heart on it, trying to keep steady as the bus moved forward.

'So, tell me how it happened again?' Katy asked Lauren, who was sitting in front of them.

'We were in Drama Club,' Lauren explained, turning round in her seat, 'and all these bees came out of the air vent in the floor!'

'I never knew she was allergic to bee stings,' Sophie

said guiltily. She added more kisses and flowers to the card, and wrote 'So SORRY you're ill!' inside it. She underlined 'SORRY' several times.

'I don't think she knew herself,' Kaz said.

'Poor Erin,' said Katy. 'Is it serious?'

'I think so,' said Joanna unhappily. 'They called an ambulance and everything.'

'Oh no ...' Katy bit her nail.

Kaz nodded. 'I know, it's terrible, isn't it?' She glanced out of the window and got up as the bus pulled up outside the hospital. 'At least your mum let us have time off school to come and see her.'

The girls found the ward where Erin was staying and the nurse looked up as they came in. 'Ah, you must be the girls from Turlingham Academy,' she said with a smile.

'Yes,' said Sophie. 'How's she doing?'

The nurse only nodded in reply. 'I'll let you have a few minutes with Erin, but you will have to be quiet. She's had a huge shock, you see.'

Sophie's heart felt like cold clay as she followed the nurse down the corridor. The nurse paused at a doorway and showed them in. Sophie put her hand to her mouth as she saw Erin lying, with her eyes closed, on the bed. She had to look twice to be sure it *was* Erin, because her face was so puffed up and sore looking. She was hooked up to a drip and she looked as if she was hardly breathing.

Katy took something out of the plastic bag she was holding. It was a collage of photos – Erin with her friends. She placed the collage on the dressing table next to the bed. Sophie added her own get-well card, and the others silently put their messages and cards next to them.

'She'll see them when she wakes up,' said Katy, her voice trembling.

'She will wake up, won't she?' Lauren said in a small, frightened voice.

'Of course she will.' Jo put an arm round Lauren.

Sophie gazed at Erin. She felt sick and shocked. *It's my fault she's so ill,* she thought, wishing she had never opened the bee book. They had to get the others out of the cubicle to see if there was anything they could do to make her better. She caught Katy's eye, and Katy nodded at once.

'I think someone should phone Mark. But we can't do it in here,' Katy suggested. 'I haven't got my phone – Kaz?'

'Of course!' Kaz headed towards the door. Lauren, who was choking back sobs, went with her, and Jo followed, still comforting Lauren.

Sophie pulled the curtain across so the bed was hidden from the ward. She was just about to speak when Katy spoke.

'It was witch magic that harmed her,' said Katy, 'so I guess we need witch hunter magic to set things right again.' She reached into her bag. 'I came prepared!'

'Great!' Sophie said, realising that Katy was probably right.

Katy held up a test tube full of a clear, sparkling liquid. She leaned over Erin and let a few drops fall onto Erin's mouth. Sophie watched as the liquid seeped between her lips. A purple aura formed over her mouth and then faded away with the liquid.

Sophie's hope ebbed away as Erin showed no sign of moving.

'It hasn't worked—'

'Wait!' Katy interrupted.

A purple aura rose up over Erin's heart and started glowing. It grew, spreading over her whole body. The swelling shrank back, and Erin's face began to look normal again.

Sophie and Katy clutched each other's hands in excitement.

The purple aura sank into Erin's body, disappearing like mist. Erin's eyelids fluttered. Her lips parted. She took a shuddering breath and sat bolt upright, gasping. Her eyes focused on the girls.

'S-Sophie?' she managed.

'Erin!' Sophie exclaimed, hugging her. Out of the corner of her eye she saw Katy smiling as she put the test tube away. *So witch hunters' magic can do good too,* she thought. The next minute she felt annoyed with herself for even thinking that. Of course witch hunters' magic could be used for good or evil, just like witch magic. It all depended on who was using it.

'W-what's happening?' Erin smiled, looking dazed. 'I was asleep. Hi, Katy.'

'Erin, I'm so glad you're awake!' Katy leaned in to hug her too. 'How are you feeling?'

'Tired ... but OK ...' Erin yawned.

'Erin!' Sophie turned round to see Kaz standing open-mouthed at the end of the bed. She pulled the curtain aside and Sophie saw the others all clustered by the door – with Mark, Callum and Oliver behind them. Mark looked pale and worried, and he was clutching a big bunch of yellow roses.

'You're better!' Kaz whooped, then pushed Mark forward. 'Mark was already getting off the bus when we called. He brought flowers ...'

Erin squealed with pleasure, and Mark blushed as he handed her the flowers. The others crowded round Erin.

'Erin, we were so worried—' Lauren burst out.

'They said you were really ill—' Jo added.

'I was so scared when you screamed!' Kaz sat down on the bed next to her.

'Oh my God, was I really loud?' Erin said.

'Yeah! I was listening to my iPod, and it was the Grease Monkeys' new song, and I actually thought the scream was on the song!' Kaz laughed.

'The *what* monkeys?' Callum said.

'Grease Monkeys. You've not heard of them?' Kaz backed out of the crush, drawing Callum with her by the arm. Katy threw a quick glance over her shoulder towards Kaz – and turned back just in time to miss Callum glancing in her direction. Sophie wished there was some way to fix this but, when it came to love, she didn't think that her magic was strong enough.

'I think you'd like them,' Kaz said to Callum, twirling her hair in her fingers as she spoke. 'Hey, do you want me to put the song on your iPod for you?'

'Um ... what?' Callum tore his gaze away from Katy. 'OK, if you like.'

'Cool!' Kaz looked delighted.

'Kids, what's this noise?' The nurse came rushing in, looking annoyed. 'Erin needs rest and – oh, my goodness!' She stared at Erin. 'You're awake!'

Erin, clutching the roses, beamed broadly. 'Yeah – I think it's the power of true love,' she said, smiling at

Mark, who went even redder. Sophie and Katy exchanged a secret grin.

The first morning of half term, Sophie and Katy were ready early. Sophie pulled her hat on and bent down to check her bag one more time.

'I've got a notebook and a pen so we can map the route,' she told Katy, 'and a packed lunch in case we're in there for a while—' Gally tugged at her sleeve. 'And some peanuts for you, Gally, don't worry!' She looked up at Katy. 'I think we're ready to explore the library!'

'Let's go!' Katy opened the door and Sophie followed her out into the autumn morning, their feet crunching on fallen leaves and frost. As they headed towards the school, Sophie heard running footsteps behind them.

'Sophie! Katy!'

It was Callum. He caught up with them, grinning hopefully. 'Hey, I heard you were staying for half term, Katy! That's really cool.'

'Yeah, I'm looking forward to it!' she said, smiling.

'I thought ... well, I thought that maybe while

you're here we could hang out?' Callum was actually bouncing up and down slightly with eagerness as he gazed at Katy.

Katy beamed and her cheeks turned pink and Sophie knew it wasn't the chilly weather. But then Katy's face fell. 'Oh ... I can't. We have to do some work. In the library.'

Callum's smile froze. 'You two seem to spend all your time in the library these days!' he said. 'Did you find that physics book you were looking for?'

'Yes,' said Katy, just as Sophie said, 'No.'

'Huh?' Callum laughed.

'We found it,' said Sophie, giving Katy a warning glance, 'but it, um, wasn't the right book after all.'

'What Sophie said,' Katy nodded, looking relieved.

'Oh, right ...' Callum looked puzzled, and there was an awkward silence. Sophie was about to say goodbye when Callum went on: 'So what have you got in that backpack, then?' He leaned round to see. 'It looks heavy – want me to carry it for you, Katy?'

'No!' Katy and Sophie burst out together. Sophie

winced as she saw Callum's hurt expression. 'Thanks,' she added, knowing it was too late. There was nothing she could do to fix things right now, she decided, and the rate she was going she would only make things worse. She took Katy's hand and pulled her away. 'Bye, Callum, see you later.'

'Bye . . . ' Callum echoed. Sophie had a last glimpse of his confused, unhappy face before the door swung shut and they were in the school.

They walked into the library and Katy sat down at one of the desks and put her head in her hands. 'Oh, that was so awful!' she said. 'I've blown it now, there's no way he'll ever like me! Did you see the look on his face?'

Sophie put down her backpack and dived into the bag. 'Don't worry, Katy,' she said firmly. 'I'm going to sort it all out.'

'You are?' Katy looked up. 'What sort of a spell is it? Are you sure—'

'It's not magic, it's technology.' Sophie pulled out her phone. 'I'm going to send him a text and tell him that you like him.'

'Sophie!' Katy lunged from her chair and grabbed at the mobile. Sophie jumped away.

'Katy, this is silly, you both really like each other!'

'Nooo! You mustn't. I'll die of embarrassment!'

Sophie rolled her eyes. 'Oh, all right then.' She slid the mobile back into her pocket.

'Thanks, Sophie.' Katy sighed. 'Anyway, I should forget about Callum. We've got more important things to worry about!'

She set off into the library, marching towards the Rare Volumes Room. As soon as her back was turned, Sophie whipped out her mobile and began texting Callum. No matter what Katy said, she knew Callum really liked her.

Katy really likes you! And I mean, likes you like THAT!!!

She pressed *send* before she could change her mind.

A second later, the phone bleeped with an answer.

Ha ha. Don't believe you. She couldn't wait to get away from me just now. Did you make her send that note?

Note? What note? thought Sophie. She slid the phone back into her pocket and hurried after Katy. The Callum problem was too complicated to deal with – he'd have to wait ...

ELEVEN

As they walked through the magic library, Sophie paused at every bookshelf to note down the number and mark it on the paper. The aisles were arranged in rows, just like in the school library, but the room was irregular and much larger, and the flickering candle-light played tricks on their eyes.

Katy glanced back. 'I'm not surprised we got lost before. I can't even see the entrance.' She shivered.

'Don't worry – we'll be fine now we have the map.' Sophie waved her notebook.

She looked at the number of the closest aisle.

'One hundred!' she said triumphantly, writing it down. 'I think we're getting closer.'

The girls went on, trying not to even glance at the books on either side until they reached the end. Sophie took a candle from a nearby sconce and shone it onto the number plate of the next aisle.

'Seventy-two,' she said in disappointment. 'We'll have to turn round and go back until we find one hundred and one.'

Katy groaned. 'We could be walking all day at this rate.' She gazed down the aisle. 'It doesn't look very long. We could just go to the end and see, couldn't we?'

They went to the end and Sophie shone the candle onto the number.

'No – this is sixty-six!' she said. 'Oh well – we can go back and start again from aisle one hundred.'

They walked back the way they had come. Sophie hesitated. Something about the aisle looked different. On impulse, she shone the candle over the number, just to check.

'But ... it doesn't say one hundred any more,' she said, confused. 'It says seventy-five! Look!'

Katy read the number and nodded. 'But how?'

'Magic, I guess!' Sophie glanced round them. She had a horrible feeling that her map was useless.

'Let's try up aisle seventy-two again,' she suggested, trying to stay positive. 'You never know – we might be lucky.'

She led the way back up the long aisle, her eyes fixed firmly in front of her. Little rustling noises sounded from the bookshelves. Suddenly from the corner of her eye she glimpsed movement – as if one of the carved owls had swooped from side to side. She gasped and glanced round. Her eye caught a title: *Rainbows of Colour*. Even though she had only read the words in her head, the book slid towards her as if a hand behind had pushed it, and fell onto the floor, open.

'Get back, Katy!' Sophie stretched out an arm to protect her. The pages of the book gave a little shake, and a dancing rainbow of colours floated out from the pages, sparkling and fluttering like butterflies.

'Oh, how beautiful!' Katy gasped. She moved forward, but Sophie pulled her back.

'I don't trust this,' she said, her eyes on the rainbow.

'But – but rainbows aren't dangerous, are they?' Katy gazed at the dancing colours.

'No,' said Sophie thoughtfully. A distant rumbling sounded from above them. 'But where there are rainbows there's always rain!'

The instant she said *rain*, there was a huge crash of thunder. Sophie and Katy screamed and clutched each other. Lightning flashed and, with a roar like a waterfall, a torrent of rain ditched itself on top of them. Sophie was drenched in a second. She grabbed Katy's hand and, holding her backpack over her head to shelter her, ran back down the aisle. The rain was freezing cold, and so heavy that it was like running through a wall of water. As they reached the end of the aisle she pulled out the map and tried to see where the exit was.

'Back this way!' she screamed over the noise of the downpour. She stuffed the map in her pocket and ran, half-blinded by the rain, along the next aisle. The bookshelves turned sharply – and ended in a wall.

'I can't run any more,' Katy panted. She slowed and halted. 'I'm soaked!'

Sophie put an arm round Katy, and shielded her face from the rain with her other hand.

'We've got to just keep looking,' she shouted over the noise of the rain. 'Who would have thought we'd need an umbrella!'

Katy managed a smile. They went on, shivering, through the puddles. Sophie noticed that despite the deluge, none of the books seemed to be getting wet.

As they walked on, the rain slowed to a drizzle, and then to a steady *drip-drip-drip*.

Sophie pushed her wet hair out of her face. 'I'm sloshing in my shoes!' she said. 'We've got to get out so we can dry off.'

'S-S-Sophie, can w-we rest f-for a bit?' Katy said through chattering teeth. 'There's a patch of sunlight over there ...'

'Yes, of course!' They hurried over to it and Katy sank gratefully to the ground. Sophie sat down next to her, and put an arm round her to keep her warm.

Gally, looking tiny and fragile with his fur all drenched, curled up in her lap.

Katy sneezed. 'I'm so . . . so tired,' she whispered.

Sophie squeezed her arm and was shocked at how cold she felt. 'Don't worry, Katy, we'll get out of here!' Sophie answered, trying not to show how worried she felt. She had to do something, but what?

There was a candle burning on the wall. It didn't give enough heat to warm them, but . . .

'Of course!' she exclaimed. She jumped up and lifted the candle from the wall. Placing it in front of them, she murmured, 'Forces of the Earth: water, wind, earth and fire – let this candle warm us like a bonfire!'

The flame stood perfectly still, and for a moment she thought it hadn't worked. Then she felt warmth moving towards her from the candle. The candle flame didn't grow bigger, but it became whiter and hotter, like a miniature sun. She sighed in relief.

'Mmm,' said Katy, moving closer to the flame. Gally turned round and round, drying every inch of his fur, then curled up and fell asleep.

'I think Gally's got the right idea,' said Katy, lying down and stretching out on the floor. 'Thanks, Sophie!' Gazing up at the ceiling, she added: 'Oh look!'

Above them was a large air vent, made of criss-crossed ironwork. There were leaves caught in the interwoven metal.

'Looks like that's the one Kaz tripped over,' she said.

'I don't know – but the ironwork has the same pattern as the symbol on the exit,' Sophie said. 'Maybe the magic runs all through the school!' She got her pen and notebook out of the backpack. 'It has to mean something,' she said, as she copied down the pattern, glancing up at it. 'I'm just not sure what . . . '

She flicked back through her notebook and found herself looking at the pieces of paper they had found: one behind the radiator in the library upstairs, the other in the envelope with the postcard in her grandma's room.

'Katy!' she cried. 'Look! The symbol in the corner here – these papers have got to be linked to the maze!'

Katy scrambled over to see. Sophie turned the papers round and round, trying to work out their meaning.

As Katy yawned and lay down again by the fire, Sophie moved the papers back and forth, turning them upside down, trying to work out what they meant. Gally hopped onto her knee as she sat cross-legged, and peered at what she was doing.

'Oh, Gally!' she said exasperatedly as she held them up to the light again. 'I just don't get it.'

She dropped the papers in despair. They drifted and shifted on the air and landed on top of each other. The symbols suddenly glowed with a warm light.

Sophie caught her breath as the papers melted into each other, becoming a single piece. The random marks merged into a single drawing as the lines matched up. The drawing was an irregular outline, all angles and corners. Inside it, lines glowed and wriggled round the paper, and tiny numbers popped up, drifting round like dust in a sunbeam.

'Oh my gosh, Katy!'

'What?' Katy sat up, looking dazed.

'It's a map of the library!' Sophie picked up the piece of paper. 'Look – the lines are the shelves, and each one has a number attached to it. But the shelves keep moving ...' The lines and numbers changed places again as she spoke, scurrying round the paper as if they were playing musical chairs. She stabbed at the paper with her finger. 'Look! There goes one hundred and thirty-eight!'

'What are we waiting for?' Katy jumped up. 'Let's go!'

They raced through the aisles, Sophie leading the way with the map in her hand. 'Quick – it went this way!'

They ran round corners and up and down corridors of books that rustled and chattered at them as they passed.

'We're gaining on it!' Sophie shouted in triumph.

'Sophie, wait!'

Sophie skidded to a halt and turned in surprise. Katy was standing still, a strange expression on her face.

'What's the matter?' Sophie looked at her.

'I ... I'm not sure,' Katy said slowly.

'Come on, then!' Sophie ran on, but stopped and turned back as she saw Katy wasn't following.

'What is it?' She headed back towards her. 'Katy? Are you all right?'

Katy crept up to her. 'I think there's another witch nearby,' she whispered.

'What do you mean? How do you know?'

'I just sense it! I'm a witch hunter, remember? You can't turn off those instincts.'

'But who is it?' Sophie's heart leapt. 'Could it be my grandma?'

'I don't know. But if they're close I can find them ... whoever they are.'

Katy slipped off her bag and searched through it, bringing out a tightly sealed spice jar with some glittery red powder in it and a small vial filled with purple liquid.

'Have we got any of those apples leftover from lunch?'

'Sure!' Sophie took her own bag off and pulled out the last apple. 'It's a bit bruised.'

'Doesn't matter.' Katy mixed some of the powder into the liquid and then dribbled it all over the apple. A purple aura trembled around it; the apple glowed a deeper red than before.

'Oh – and you should touch that magnet,' Katy added, looking up at Sophie. 'Or the formula will just find you!'

Sophie hastily turned her bracelet over. 'It's not . . . dangerous, is it?' she asked.

Katy shook her head as she chanted. '*Umbra aut luce, die aut nocte* . . . let the witch come to sight!'

She stood up and rolled the apple down the aisle as if it were a bowling ball. Sophie watched as the apple trundled, glowing, into the shadows. But just as she was expecting it to slow down and stop, it picked up speed.

'Follow it!' Katy grabbed her bag and broke into a run.

Sophie raced after her. The apple rumbled on ahead, swerving round corners and down aisles. As Sophie ran, she heard a noise – distant singing.

'Can you hear that?' she gasped to Katy.

Katy nodded. 'It sounds like a woman . . . '

The singing was getting closer now, and there was something in the tone of the voice that made Sophie shiver. At times, it went off into wild shrieks that seemed torn with despair. She glanced at the shelves, worried that another strange book was ready to leap out at them.

The apple rolled round the corner. They ran after it – and skidded to a halt.

The apple had stopped in the middle of the aisle. A tall woman was bending over it. She wore boots with long pointed toes and flowing skirts in many different colours. Her brown hair looked as if it hadn't been brushed for weeks. Sophie did a double take as she saw a shining green lizard in it, then realised it was a jade hairslide.

As the woman examined the apple she exclaimed: 'Ha!' and did a strange little stamping dance that made her skirts billow round like clouds.

There was something wrong about this woman, Sophie thought – something threatening. She jerked her head back, mouthing, 'Let's go,' to Katy. Katy nodded and they tiptoed backwards. But as they turned to run, the woman's voice rang out behind them ...

'Stop!'

TWELVE

'Please stop!'

The woman's voice was so terrified and pleading that Sophie turned round. She saw her running towards them, arms outstretched. The woman flung herself at their feet. She was half laughing and half crying.

'Oh, thank you – thank you so much for rescuing me!' she cried.

Sophie looked at Katy, who looked as puzzled as she felt. 'What do you mean, rescuing you?' She reached out a hand to help the woman up – but she leapt to her feet. Her eyes widened with terror.

'No! Keep back! It's him—!' She pointed into the shadows. Sophie swung round, her heart leaping in panic, but there was no one there.

The woman let out a wild giggle, then clapped a hand over her mouth. Her shoulders shook with silent laughter, which turned suddenly to jerky sobs.

'The shadows – the books – they're laughing at me!' she whimpered.

Sophie hesitated, caught between pity and fear. The woman seemed mad. Maybe she was another demagicked witch – like her grandmother. Being demagicked could drive witches insane.

'C-calm down,' she said. 'What's happened to you? You can tell us – we won't hurt you.'

The woman hiccupped out something between a laugh and a sob.

'I've been trapped in here for weeks! No – it must be only days – but it feels so much longer.' She put a hand to her head. 'I don't know how I survived – I've been wandering back and forth, until I thought I would go mad—'

'What happened? Did you get in here by mistake?' Sophie asked.

The woman shook her head. 'No, I was browsing for books. I became trapped and couldn't find my way out. I've been down here so long, in the shadows, all alone . . . I thought I would never get out! Thank you – thank you again.' She swept them a low curtsey. 'My name is Angelica, and I will always remember that you saved my life.'

'We're glad we could!' said Sophie. 'I'm Sophie – and this is Katy. But how did you get trapped? Did you get lost in the aisles?'

'It's a terrible story.' Angelica shook her head sadly. 'An evil man, a witch, tricked me. He cursed the library so that the aisles would all move round, and I would never find my way out.'

'An evil witch?' Sophie raised her eyebrows. 'But I thought – I didn't know there were such things.' She had been about to say: *I thought only witch hunters could be evil*, but then she remembered Katy was standing next to her.

Angelica smiled at her but the smile didn't reach

her eyes. 'My dear, witches – *and* witch hunters – can be either bad or good.'

Sophie had never had that thought before: that witches could be bad. For so long she thought that witches were good and witch hunters were bad. Now she realised she'd been naïve; it wasn't as simple as that.

'Just like humans,' added Angelica.

'That's terrible,' said Katy, stepping towards Angelica. 'Do you know the witch who did this to you?'

The woman gave a brief laugh. 'Oh yes. His name is Franklin Poulter.'

Angelica's words hit Sophie so hard that she wanted to hit back. 'No!' she gasped. 'How dare you? I don't believe you!'

The room spun before her eyes. Katy caught her arm and steadied her before she could fall.

'Sophie – Sophie, are you OK?'

'She's lying,' she said. 'Franklin Poulter would never do anything evil!' She turned back to Angelica, ready to retort, but the look of tender pity in the witch's eyes stopped her. 'My father wouldn't—'

'Your father!' Now Angelica looked shocked. She was silent for a moment before her face relaxed and she tilted her head to the side. 'Poor child,' she said. 'You're like me – you want to believe the best of people. But . . . ' She threw a sharp, wild glance over her shoulder into the shadows. 'I *saw* him do it. Franklin Poulter stood before me as he placed a curse on this library and trapped me.' She gulped down a sob.

'Wait – you mean he was right here?' Katy asked. 'In the school?'

Angelica nodded.

'That's not true!' Sophie cried. Her heart ached. Surely her father couldn't have come here, to the school – so close to her – and not tried to see her.

'Oh,' Angelica said, reaching out to stroke Sophie's hair but Sophie stepped away from her. 'I know you want to trust and love your father . . . but do you really know the true Franklin Poulter?'

'I – he – he's been in hiding,' Sophie faltered. 'He's been gone for years.'

'He never mentioned a child,' Angelica said, and this time when she reached out for Sophie's hand she allowed her to take it. 'Does he really care about you?'

'H-he was trying to protect us . . . ' She tailed off when she saw Katy wincing. 'You don't believe her, do you? Katy!'

'The thing is, Sophie . . . ' Katy said soberly, 'you don't know much about him. All you've heard about him is from your grandmother, isn't it? And – well – she's his mother.'

Angelica dropped Sophie's hand and turned away abruptly so her face was in shadow. Sophie didn't reply. She could see how terribly possible it was. Of course Grandma wouldn't say anything bad about her own son . . .

She shook her head. 'It must be a misunderstanding,' she said. 'Angelica, tell me exactly what happened.'

Angelica shrank away, her eyes white and wild. 'I can't. I can't. Please don't ask me to relive it.'

She flattened herself against the bookshelves, clawing at the books as if at the walls of a prison.

Katy tugged Sophie's sleeve. 'Sophie, let's not push her,' she whispered.

Sophie swallowed. Katy was right – it wasn't fair. 'It's OK. We won't talk about it any more,' she said gently to Angelica. She searched for a way to change the subject. 'We – we're looking for a book. A magic book. We found it upstairs, but now it's on aisle one hundred and thirty-eight.'

'Aisle one hundred and thirty-eight!' Angelica froze, then drew in her breath as if they had said it was on the top of Everest. Slowly, she smiled. 'Well, I will use my witchcraft to help you find the book if you can help me get out of here.'

'Of course we'll help you get out,' Sophie said. 'But we don't need your help to find the book, thanks all the same – we have a map.'

Angelica laughed. 'Do you know how big that aisle is? You *will* need my help, once we get there.'

Sophie glanced at Katy. There didn't seem any harm in her coming with them, and they couldn't leave her alone in the maze. Katy shrugged and nodded.

'OK then,' Sophie said with a weak smile. 'Let's go.' Gally scampered onto Sophie's shoulder and sat there, looking at Angelica. Angelica smiled and reached out a hand to ruffle his ears.

'What a sweet familiar,' she said. 'And where's yours, Katy?'

'Oh, I ... don't have one,' said Katy. 'I'm not a witch.' She met Sophie's eyes.

'Well, I'm afraid that I have no imagination at all – I went for the classic choice.' Angelica turned round and whistled into the shadows. 'Come along, Mincing! Where are you?'

A sleek Siamese cat came prowling through the shadows. It wrapped itself round Angelica's legs, looking up at the girls with shining green eyes.

'She's beautiful,' said Sophie. The cat purred.

'And doesn't she know it!' Angelica laughed.

Sophie laughed too. She felt that she liked the woman. She was odd – but not really mad, she decided. Just eccentric, and disturbed by her imprisonment. But if Angelica wasn't mad . . . what did that say about her father?

As she was thinking, a yawning dark valley seemed to open up ahead of them. She paused and glanced at the number on the bookshelf.

'Aisle one hundred and thirty-eight!' she exclaimed. The bookshelf towered above her, its highest shelf dizzyingly lost in the shadows. She turned to Angelica. 'You were right – it really is huge!'

In silent awe, they stepped into the aisle. The far end was invisible in the distance. There was a thick hush over everything, and a smell of ancient paper.

Katy cupped her hand round her mouth and shouted, 'Hello!' A few moments later, her voice echoed back to her.

'Wow,' Sophie murmured.

Angelica flexed her knuckles, stretched out her hands and ran them along the air, as if she were playing an invisible harp. Sophie wondered where her Source was – and then saw the jade lizard hairslide glittering and glowing in the half-light, its red eyes shining as if it were alive.

Angelica's lips moved silently. A moment later, something came swooping down the aisle like a bird. It thumped to the floor at Angelica's feet.

'*Magic Most Dark*!' Sophie squealed in delight, bending to pick up the heavy, leather-bound book. The clasps grinned at her.

Katy craned over her shoulder as Sophie turned the pages. They flicked through the pages; the title of every spell was written in beautiful calligraphy at the top of each: *A Spell to Enslave the Unwary*; A *Spell to Muddle and Befuddle*; *A Spell to Break Hearts*.

'It's definitely dark magic,' said Sophie.

'Yes . . . but this is interesting stuff,' Katy said, placing a hand on the book to stop Sophie turning the page. 'Look – it says here that gold shields witch hunters from witches! I never knew that.'

Sophie scanned down the slanting writing. 'Here it is!' she cried. '*A Spell to Find Any Named Witch*.' She ran her finger along the words. As she did so, something fell out of the back of the book. It was a postcard. There was nothing written on it, but when she turned it over, her heart sank. It was the same as the one they'd found in her grandmother's room – a picture of Durham Cathedral on the front. This postcard was blank but that one had been signed with an F – for Franklin.

Sophie stared down at the postcard, not wanting to believe her eyes. Had her father used *Magic Most Dark* to cast evil spells, to capture and enslave people – people like Angelica?

'Look at this,' she said, her voice wobbling as she showed the postcard to Katy and Angelica. *Maybe my father is a bad witch after all,* she thought.

Angelica nodded sadly, and laid a hand on Sophie's shoulder. Mincing sidled up and rubbed against her ankles with a mew.

Sophie closed the book and held it to her chest. 'Do you think he could have harmed my grandma?' she said. 'I don't want to believe it, but ... '

'Oh, Sophie, don't jump to conclusions,' Katy said, putting an arm round her.

'You're right.' Sophie sighed.

'Why don't we take the book back with us?' Katy suggested. 'It would be easier to cast the spell outside the library.' She took the book from Sophie and examined the spell. 'It looks very complicated!'

They headed to the end of the aisle. As she stepped out of it, the book tingled in Sophie's hands, and leapt out of her grasp as if it had been hooked by an invisible fisherman.

'Huh?' Sophie bent to pick the book up again. But when she tried to walk on, the book pulled itself out of her hands once more.

'It must be enchanted,' Angelica told them. 'There's a spell stopping the book from leaving the aisle.'

'Oh.' Sophie opened the book. 'Well, I guess we have to cast the spell right here.'

Katy glanced at her watch. 'It's nearly seven oclock. Your mum will be looking for us if we're not careful. Let's come back tomorrow and study the spell some more.'

'I suppose you're right,' Sophie sighed. She carefully put the book back on the shelf, facing out so it was easy to find again. She was glad she had her friend with her. She wasn't thinking clearly after the shock of what she'd heard: her father had been less than a hundred metres away from her and hadn't come to see her. Sophie wasn't sure her dad was the type of witch she liked.

'Thank you so much for helping me,' Angelica said as they left the school building. 'I don't know if I would have ever escaped without you!'

Sophie smiled at her. 'You're welcome.'

'It's a real shame to say goodbye.' Angelica stroked Sophie's hair. 'You're a very sweet girl.'

'Thanks,' Sophie said. To her surprise, she felt sorry to be saying goodbye to Angelica too. It felt as if they had known each other for ages . . .

She waved, and headed off with Katy. As she did so, Angelica's last words reached her.

'And I'm sorry about your father – sorry that you had to find out the truth this way.'

Sophie's smile faltered. She raised her hand in a wave and hurried on without looking back.

THIRTEEN

'This is the best and *warmest* soup I've ever tasted!' said Katy with a happy sigh. 'Thanks so much, Mrs Morrow.'

'Yes, thanks, Mum!' Sophie dunked a piece of bread into her tomato and meatball soup. 'But aren't you going to have any?'

'I'm not hungry,' Sophie's mum answered, pulling her gaze away from the window. She gave the girls a tired smile. 'So, what did you do today?'

Sophie caught Katy's eye. 'Just . . . went for a walk.'

'Oh ... good.' Sophie's mum stood up abruptly and walked to the window. 'There'll be a frost tonight,' she said as if to herself.

'Did you hear anything else about Grandma?' she asked.

Her mother shook her head, and Sophie saw tears in her eyes. 'I can't bear to think of her out there – alone, confused, and in the cold.' She turned back to the window.

And perhaps in danger from witch hunters, Sophie thought.

Katy put down her spoon and placed a comforting hand on hers. Sophie blinked her tears away. She didn't want her mother to see how upset she was – it would only worry her more.

She made up her mind. She *had* to get hold of *Magic Most Dark,* that very evening. She couldn't rest while Grandma was still missing. She glanced at Katy. Maybe, she thought, she could kill two birds with one stone.

'Mum ... could Katy and I go and see a movie at Callum's tonight?'

'That's a good idea.' Her mother turned round, smiling and dabbing her eyes. 'You should do something to relax, take your mind off things.'

'Are you sure he won't mind us inviting ourselves over?' Katy said.

Sophie rolled her eyes. 'Hmm ... let's see what he says, shall we?'

She texted Callum quickly. A second later her phone bleeped with his answer:

Brilliant! You and Katy are welcome ANY TIME ☺

Sophie grinned at Katy. 'Now, how did I know he would say that?'

Sophie and Katy crossed the courtyard towards Callum's house, dry leaves scuttling ahead of them on the wind. As they walked, Katy glanced into the shadows.

'What's the matter, Katy?' Sophie asked eventually.

Katy sighed. 'Angelica creeped me out a little bit. Didn't you think she was odd?'

'Well, she had been stuck in a maze for a week or more,' Sophie pointed out. 'You wouldn't be normal either if that had happened to you.' She sighed. 'I know she said bad things about my father, but I felt – I don't know – I kind of liked her.'

'Hmm,' said Katy thoughtfully.

They reached the door of Callum's cottage. Sophie reached up and hammered the knocker. Then she gave Katy a cheeky look and stepped back from the door. 'Well, have fun!'

'Huh?' Katy gaped at her. 'Where are you going? What about Callum?'

'I'm sure he'll enjoy the movie even more if it's just the two of you!'

Katy's look of confusion turned into a blush as she realised what was going on. 'Oh no! Sophie!' She caught her arm. 'You can't just leave me!'

Sophie wriggled out of her grip, laughing. 'You'll have a great time. Besides, I don't want to get in the way of my two best friends' romance.' She ran off down the path, just as Callum opened the front door.

'Hi, guys – come on in!' He grinned at Katy.

Katy smiled back through her blushes.

'Uh – I left something at home, Callum,' Sophie

called from the gate. 'You go ahead and start without me!'

She ran off towards the school building, chuckling to herself.

Sophie's footsteps echoed as she walked through the secret library. She had the map in her hand – but even so, the long, gloomy aisles were scarier than she thought they'd be.

'Glad you're here, Gally,' she whispered to the squirrel, who was riding in her pocket. His ears pricked up at the sound of her voice.

Sophie reached aisle one hundred and thirty-eight and went straight to the place where she had left the book. It took her a single glance to see it wasn't there.

'Oh no!'

Sophie searched all along the shelf, even kneeling down to look underneath in case it had fallen. It was nowhere to be seen. Her heart racing, she tried the other shelves. Gally leapt from her pocket and scaled the bookshelves that were out of her reach, swinging and jumping from one to the other. The books rustled angrily as he scampered over them, pausing and clinging onto them to check the spines.

Sophie found books about controlling tides and raising mountains, books about enchanted waterfalls and bewitched lighthouses – but not *Magic Most Dark*. And if she couldn't find the book ... she wouldn't be able to find Grandma.

Gally came leaping down the shelves and Sophie caught him. He had nothing in his paws.

'It really has gone!' Sophie groaned. She looked up at the shelves. She hated to disturb Katy and Callum – but this was an emergency.

She pulled out her phone and texted Katy:

Help! The book's gone. Meet me at the library in 5

'Maybe a witch hunter will do better, Gally,' she sighed, bending to pick up her bag. As she leaned down, she noticed mud on the floor. Sophie stared. The mud was ridged as if it had come from the sole of a boot. She looked up the aisle. More clods of mud were scattered in front of her. They were evenly spaced like footsteps.

Slinging her bag on her shoulder, Sophie began to run, following the footprints. The prints were pointy.

They led her up and down the aisles, and finally came to a dead end in a corner. She spun round. They couldn't just have vanished . . .

Her gaze fell on a candle lying on the floor, burnt almost to the ground. Suddenly she realised where she was – in the dead end where they had stopped to rest after the rain. Which meant that above her was . . .

'The air vent! It's open!'

Something glinted at her feet. Sophie bent to pick it up and found a piece of twisted metal.

Gally scampered across to Sophie, carrying another, similar, metal piece. Sophie took the two pieces of metal and turned them round until they fitted into each other.

The solid metal seemed to have been simply blown apart – twisted and burned by a great force. Her heart sank. She could almost see it happening before her eyes: Angelica breaking the vent open with a spell, then climbing out with the book and walking away through the woods.

Using the map to guide her, Sophie rushed back through the library, up the stairs to the entrance. Gally bounded alongside her. She put her hands on the two panels and forced them together. They slotted into place, forming the symbol, and the door grated open.

Katy was standing on the other side, her cheeks pink as if she had been running.

Sophie panted as she spoke. 'How did it go? Did he ask you out? Did he kiss you?' Sophie's voice faltered as she saw Katy's expression. 'Oh no – what happened?'

'Well . . . he'd just put his arm round me, and then I got your text. I had to leave . . . He thought I was making an excuse!'

'Oh no!' Sophie said apologetically. 'Oh, Katy – I'm so sorry. I could kick myself!'

Katy forced a smile. 'Never mind. The most important thing is the book, isn't it? If it's gone, how will we find your Grandma?'

'I don't know. It looks like you were right – Angelica tricked us!'

Sophie's instinct to trust the witch had been completely wrong.

FOURTEEN

'No way!' Katy looked horrified. 'I wouldn't dare, Sophie! What if he said no?' She hugged her legs. They were in their pyjamas, sitting on Sophie's bed as the morning sun streamed in through the window. They had gone over the events of yesterday so many times that there was nothing else to think about. The book was gone. Angelica had taken it. They would not be able to find Grandma. Her father was an evil witch.

What Sophie needed now was to think about something normal. Like Katy's crush.

'He's not going to say no – I told you a million times, he really likes you,' Sophie said.

Katy twisted a strand of her hair round her finger. 'I wouldn't dare ask him out face to face.'

'No need!' Sophie jumped up and got her lap top off the desk. 'Callum always logs on first thing in the morning.'

She tapped in her password. Callum's Elfin Warriors avatar was on the screen.

'See, told you – he's online!' She passed the computer over to Katy. 'Off you go. Just tell him you're sorry you had to leave the other night and can you meet up later today.'

'If you're sure . . . ' Katy muttered.

Hi Callum, it's Katy she typed, wincing.

Hi Katy! flashed up the response.

I'm really sorry I had to leave last night. Katy hesitated. Sophie gave her a stern look. Katy gulped and typed in. *Would you like to meet up later today instead?*

She had hardly pressed return when the answer flew onto the screen.

Yes! And a second later. *Where & when?*

Katy yelped in delight.

'Told you!' Sophie laughed. She turned away from the computer screen to let Katy have some privacy. It was great that she was managing to get Katy and Callum together, she thought. Because nothing else was working! She had no idea how to get the book back – or how to find Angelica. And even though Katy kept telling her not to blame herself, she was scared that trusting Angelica had put her grandma in even worse danger.

'I'm ready!' Sophie said, fastening the last button on her coat. She smiled at her friend. 'Katy – you look gorgeous!'

'Honestly?' Katy glanced quickly in the hall mirror.

'Callum's not going to know what hit him, I promise.' Sophie studied Katy's face, feeling as excited as if it was her going on a date. 'Ooh – I know.' She searched through her bag and pulled out her favourite peach lip-gloss. 'The finishing touch!' she said, handing it to Katy. 'He won't be able to resist kissing you!'

Katy blushed. 'I hope so!' She put on the lip-gloss and Sophie beamed; Katy looked even prettier, if that was possible. She reached for the door handle.

'I can't believe how scary this is,' Katy groaned. 'Can you do that jasmine spell you did for Erin?!'

'You don't need it! You just have to relax. Take a deep breath,' Sophie told her. Katy inhaled obediently. 'Now let it out. Feel better?'

Katy nodded and bounced up and down on the tips of her toes. 'OK – bring it on!'

Sophie opened the door and they went out into the misty evening. As they crossed the courtyard Sophie saw Callum coming towards them. Even at this distance she could tell he had brushed his hair. *A good start*, she thought, grinning to herself. She raised her hand and waved. Callum beamed and Sophie, glancing at Katy, was delighted to see she was wearing a huge, if nervous smile.

'Sophie!' came a shout from behind them. 'Katy!'

Sophie turned round, startled. Her mother was at the door of the cottage, waving urgently. She had a phone in her other hand.

'Come back here, please!' Sophie's mum called.

Sophie's shoulders slumped.

'Oh no – what bad timing,' she sighed. 'Well, we'd better see what she wants.'

She waved to Callum and pointed back to their mother. Callum nodded.

They ran back to the cottage. By the time they reached the door, Sophie's mum had disappeared into the house.

'Mum?' Sophie called.

'Oh, Sophie!' Her mother came down the stairs. She was still grasping the phone, but to Sophie's astonishment she was carrying Katy's suitcase as well.

'Mum! What's going on?'

Her mother dropped the suitcase at the bottom of the stairs.

'I've heard from the police – there's been a sighting of Grandma, in Scotland, of all places!' She shook her head. 'I've called my cousin in Edinburgh and she can put me up—'

'Scotland?' Sophie exclaimed. Of course, she reminded herself, it could be a false alarm . . .

'Yes! Sophie, you'll have to stay at Katy's house.' Sophie's mum turned and raced back up the stairs.

Sophie nodded, then caught Katy's eye. Katy looked horrified. She clapped a hand to her mouth as she realised what her mother's plans meant: she was going to have to stay under the same roof as the Gibsons for an entire week!

'But – but—' she began. 'Can't I come with you?'

Her mother came back down again with another suitcase. 'I'm sorry, honey – but there is really no alternative.'

'But, Mum . . . ' Sophie began. Even if she hadn't had to go to Katy's house, there was so much to do at Turlingham! She needed to find Angelica; she needed to get *Magic Most Dark* back. And she had to find out if her father was truly a bad witch. But she couldn't tell her mum any of that . . .

'It's fine! I've already arranged it all.' Sophie's mum glanced at her watch. 'There's a train in an hour. Sophie, I've tossed some clean clothes in a bag for you. Run upstairs and grab anything else you want to take, but be quick about it. We have to leave in a few minutes. Katy, you should go up too and check I haven't missed any-thing of yours.'

Sophie hesitated for a second, but there was nothing she could do. She ran upstairs. Katy followed. As soon as the bedroom door was shut, she turned to Katy.

'This is a nightmare!' she said. 'Your parents are totally going to find out that I'm a witch. *Ashton* will be there! I can't go, Katy!'

'I don't think we've got any choice,' Katy said. She bit her nail. 'Sophie, don't worry. I'll make sure you're safe.'

Sophie's mum called up the stairs.

'Taxi's here, girls! Hurry up or we'll miss the train!'

They raced down the stairs, and followed Sophie's mother into the taxi. As it drove away, Katy gasped: 'Oh no!'

'Did you forget something?' Sophie asked.

'Yes – Callum!' Katy pulled out her phone. 'I'll text him and try to explain.'

Sophie looked out of the window. Callum was standing, looking lost and confused, in the middle of the courtyard, watching the taxi drive away. Her heart sank – on top of everything else, it was starting to look as if her two best friends would never get together!

FIFTEEN

Mrs Gibson felt in her handbag and pulled out her keys. She turned to smile at Sophie, and revealed the terrible scar that warped the other side of her face. Even though Sophie had seen it before it still took her by surprise.

'Welcome to our little home!' she said.

Sophie managed a weak smile, clutching the handle of her suitcase. The house was more of a mansion, painted gleaming white with glossy black beams, and surrounded by neatly mown grass. She glanced at Katy for reassurance, but Katy didn't meet her eye.

She had been oddly quiet ever since Mrs Gibson had picked the girls up from the station – speaking only when her mother spoke to her.

Mrs Gibson unlocked the front door and ushered them in. Sophie edged inside, trying not to touch anything. She hadn't imagined the house of a witch hunter would be like this. It was normal ... too normal. There didn't seem to be a hair on the carpet or a speck of dust on the occasional tables. Sophie thought of her own home, of the piles of ironing and shoes cast off around the foot of the stairs, of the stain where she'd dropped a cup of Ribena on the carpet. Katy's house was impressive – but it looked as if no one was allowed to live in it.

'Do come through to the living room.' Mrs Gibson ushered them in. Sophie went, trembling. She glanced at her friendship bracelet to reassure herself that the magnet was touching her skin.

'Won't you sit down?' Mrs Gibson turned to Katy. 'Fetch some orange juice, would you, darling. Sophie must be thirsty.' It sounded more like an order than a request.

Katy slipped away. Sophie was glad to sit; she felt as if she was going to collapse at any moment. She perched herself on the edge of a beautiful creamy white sofa, hoping she wouldn't get any dirt on it. She wondered what she would do if Mr and Mrs Gibson tried to demagick her. Being demagicked could send her mad, like her grandmother. But if she resisted, they might simply kill her.

'You poor dear, are you cold?' Mrs Gibson sat down herself, right next to Sophie. 'I saw you trembling.' She put an arm round Sophie's shoulders. Sophie tensed up with terror.

Katy came through the door carrying a tray with orange juice on it. She hastily put it down as she caught Sophie's expression. 'I think Sophie's tired,' she said. 'Shall I show her to her room?'

Sophie nodded gratefully. Mrs Gibson smiled and let her go. 'What a good idea. Katy, I am glad to see you being such a good hostess. Off you go, then. Sleep well.'

'I will,' Sophie lied.

*

As soon as Katy had shut the bedroom door behind them, Sophie put down her suitcase and collapsed on the bed with a sigh of relief.

'Sophie, I'm so sorry about this,' Katy whispered, glancing nervously at the door. 'But don't worry – I'm looking out for you. I'll make sure she doesn't suspect a thing.'

'Thank you so much,' Sophie whispered.

'So long as you keep your friendship bracelet the right way round, you'll be perfectly safe,' Katy told her. She glanced round the room, frowning.

'Is there anything else you need?' she said, sounding like her mother for a moment. 'There are towels on the bed and extra blankets in the wardrobe.'

Sophie glanced round. The room was decorated in pink and white. The pillowcases matched the wallpaper and the towels were monogrammed with a big G for Gibson. 'It's . . . lovely.'

Katy laughed, sounding more like herself. 'No, it's not – it's cold and soulless,' she said.

'Can't I stay in your room?' Sophie asked.

'No, I'm sorry,' Katy said. 'Mum always insists that

guests have their own room – she believes that a good night's sleep is the most important thing in the world.'

'Oh, OK.'

'Actually, Mum might have a point,' Katy studies Sophie's face. 'You look like you could do with a rest.'

Sophie nodded, she felt exhausted.

'I'll leave you to it.'

As Sophie lay in bed she felt more lonely and afraid than she had ever done in her life before. She got up and put a chair under the handle of the door, just in case. She was tiptoeing back to bed when she heard a scratching at the window, and froze. Half of her wanted to run back to bed and put the covers over her head, but the other half told her that if the sound was coming from outside the house, it was unlikely to be the Gibsons. She opened the curtains and peeked out. In the moonlight she saw an unhappy, shivering little shape perched on the windowsill.

'Gally!' Sophie flung open the window. He must have managed to slip into the car. 'You're so brave!'

Gally hesitated on the edge, clearly not happy about going into the house.

'Oh, you poor thing,' Sophie murmured. She let Gally leap into her arms and hurried back to bed with him. Gally snuggled up to her finger, and quickly drifted off to sleep.

The third time Sophie opened her eyes, her bedside clock said 6a.m. Too early to get up – but she couldn't bear to stay in bed any longer.

She pulled out her phone and texted her mum.

Any news about Grandma?

The reply pinged back instantly; Sophie guessed that her mother couldn't sleep either.

Not yet. It's not looking hopeful, no further sightings. Try not to worry.

Sophie sighed. So her grandma wasn't found – and there was no chance of her getting away from the Gibsons early.

She tiptoed out of the door, towards the bathroom. On the landing she heard voices, echoing up from the ground floor. She shivered as she realised that one was Ashton's – and then she heard her own name.

'I *know* Sophie's a witch,' he said. 'I'm sure of it.'

Sophie edged down the stairs. At the bottom she stopped, and listened. The voices were coming from behind a door to her right. It was almost shut – but not quite.

Hardly daring to breathe, Sophie edged towards it, and pushed it gently with her finger. The door opened a crack more.

Mr Gibson was sitting at the opposite side of a huge, wooden desk, spread with papers. Sophie could see Mrs Gibson seated to one side of him. She didn't look happy and Sophie wasn't surprised: the room didn't live up to her neatness standards! There were old, dusty maps hanging on the wall, and strange objects all round the room – an African mask; a globe that showed star maps instead of continents; an ancient-looking helmet made of greenish metal.

'She can't be a witch,' Mr Gibson said, his voice a deep rumble. His eyebrows were bushy and he had a craggy, dark face. 'We've already tested her.'

'Do use your head,' Mrs Gibson snapped. 'Katy would know if her friend was a witch!' Her voice dropped another couple of degrees. 'Are you suggesting a Gibson would betray her own family? And bring a witch to stay under their very roof?'

'It's a serious accusation,' Mr Gibson growled.

Sophie cringed inside. She had thought she was the one in danger, but Katy was running just as big a risk.

'Well ... perhaps we shouldn't miss the opportunity to make sure Katy hasn't been tricked,' said Mr Gibson. 'But the burden of proof is on you, Ashton. See what you can find out about this Morrow girl.'

Sophie backed away. She had heard enough to know she was in big trouble.

At breakfast, Sophie pushed her toast round her plate, trying to look as if she was eating. Her stomach was full of butterflies and there was no room for food. Ashton wasn't there but Mr Gibson was terrifying enough, sitting at the far end of the table, frowning into his newspaper.

She glanced at Katy, but before she could catch her eye, Mrs Gibson spoke.

'Katy, dear, the car seems to be playing up and we really need some milk. Would you mind heading into town for me and picking some up, please?' she asked, spearing a slice of fruit with her fork.

'Oh, OK. No problem,' said Katy. 'Sophie, we can go to my favourite hot chocolate place while we're down there.'

'Oh, but Sophie has had such a difficult time lately,' Mrs Gibson cut in. 'I think a trip into town would be far too tiring for her.'

Sophie almost choked on her toast at the thought of being trapped alone with the Gibsons. 'Honestly, I'm fine—'

'But I can see how pale you are,' Mrs Gibson interrupted with a tight smile. 'No, much better that you stay here.'

Sophie didn't dare protest.

As they carried their plates to the dishwasher, Katy whispered to her: 'I'll be as quick as I can! Just stay away from Ashton and everything will be fine.'

Sophie managed a smile.

'Come on, Katy!' Mrs Gibson called.

Katy gave Sophie hug for luck and ran out of the kitchen door.

Sophie hurried up to her bedroom. From the window, she looked down and saw Katy walking away. Sophie waved but Katy didn't see her. She sighed and moved away from the window, lying down on her bed and staring at the ceiling.

Five minutes later, there was a knock on the bedroom door. Sophie got up and opened it.

Mrs Gibson stood outside. 'I don't know what we were thinking,' she said. 'Why would you want to be stuck inside on a lovely autumn day like this?'

Sophie's hopes rose.

'You can go to that hot chocolate place Katy loves so much.'

'Thanks, Mrs Gibson!' Sophie said, already salivating at the thought of creamy hot chocolate.

'Ashton will take you there,' Mrs Gibson added.

And now her hopes were dashed again. This was all part of their plan. Sophie thought about saying she didn't want to go but one look at Mrs Gibson's expression told her that it wouldn't work. Besides, as scary as Ashton was, he wasn't as scary as his parents. She went slowly downstairs. Ashton was already waiting there, looking as groomed and annoyingly handsome as always with a smirk on his face. Sophie avoided his eyes as she put her coat and hat on.

'Enjoy yourselves, you two,' Mrs Gibson said sweetly, and shut the door behind them so hard that it rattled the glass in the windows.

Ashton led Sophie across the main road and in through the iron gates of a park. It was full of beautiful old trees, and the fallen leaves were crusted with frost. There were other people around, cycling or jogging or walking their dogs. Sophie couldn't help thinking how ironic it was. Anyone seeing her and Ashton together would think they were boyfriend and girlfriend – which couldn't have been further from the truth.

'Penny for your thoughts,' said Ashton, with a grin.

Sophie blushed. 'N-nothing much,' she stammered.

'I was just thinking,' said Ashton, kicking at the leaves as they walked, 'that we never got to finish our very interesting conversation the other day.'

'I don't remember,' said Sophie.

'Come on, Sophie,' he said, half-threatening and half-persuasive. 'Don't play games with me. Who's this "*her*" you were talking about?'

Sophie didn't have to fake her anger as she replied, 'My grandma. And she's missing, if you remember – so I'd appreciate it if you stopped asking stupid questions.'

'Yeah, course. So sorry about that,' Ashton said, not sounding sorry at all. 'But isn't there someone else on your father's side? Another woman, for example?'

Sophie's heart jumped. Did Ashton know about her father's long-lost sister, Gertrude? But she was sure it was only her and Katy who'd seen it on the birth certificate. She hoped Gertrude was safe ... wherever she was.

'I don't know what you're talking about,' she said, and increased her pace.

'Course you do. Come on, Sophie. Spill the beans.'

Sophie stared at the ground and strode on, faster.

'Sophie ... ' he said behind her. 'You know I'll find out sooner or later.'

Not if I have anything to do with it, thought

Sophie, but she pressed her lips together and ignored him.

Her tactic seemed to work: he sighed and stopped asking questions. Grateful for the silence, Sophie walked on.

The path led them down a slope and into a thicket of dark pine trees. It was suddenly dark, and quiet except for the crunch of their steps on the gravel.

Ashton frowned as he strode on, glancing into the trees. 'These woods are just like the ones in *Full Moon*,' he said, suddenly, almost as if he was talking to himself.

'Um, yeah – you're right,' said Sophie, warily.

'Oh, you've seen that film?' Ashton turned to her enthusiastically. 'What did you think?'

Sophie was startled. She realised she had never thought of Ashton as liking werewolf films, or liking, well, anything except trying to scare her to death.

'I loved it! I mean, Jareth Quinn's in it – and he's gorgeous . . . '

She broke off, blushing furiously as she caught Ashton's eye. She had been concentrating so hard on not giving herself away that she'd completely forgotten that Ashton looked very similar to her favourite actor. She realised that his leather jacket was like the one Jareth had worn in *Full Moon* – and yes, he even had his hair styled the same way.

Ashton laughed. 'Katy's the clever one. Everyone knows that.' He sounded bitter, and Sophie remembered the dismissive way his parents had spoken to him that morning. 'The only thing I've got going for me is that I look a little bit like a film star.' He gave her a wry grin, then glanced away, looking a little embarrassed.

Sophie was startled to find herself wanting to reassure him. She gave herself a little shake. There was no way she could trust Ashton. He was probably just trying to get her to talk.

Well, I won't, she thought. *He can answer the questions for once!*

'It must be tough not being the favourite,' she said.

'It is.' Sophie was surprised at the energy in his voice. 'I mean, it's not my fault I'm not talented like

Katy! I try, but . . . ' He shook his head. 'It's never enough.'

Sophie couldn't think of a word to say in reply. For a second, she thought he looked even more handsome than Jareth Quinn. But the next moment he tensed, and his green eyes focused on something in the distance. A figure in a red coat was heading towards them. It was Katy.

'Oh, great, here comes the witch-lover,' Ashton said, and the anger in his voice was back.

'Ashton, don't be ridiculous,' said Sophie.

But Ashton just turned his back on her. 'You two deserve each other.'

He turned on his heel and strode off through the trees, leaving Sophie speechless.

SIXTEEN

'I just wish there was something I could do,' Katy said as Sophie closed the bedroom door behind her. 'But since your grandma's already been demagicked, it'll be even harder to find her.'

Sophie glanced round at Katy's bedroom, clutching the Gibsons's atlas to her chest. The room was much bigger than her own, but much less cosy. It looked as if Mrs Gibson, not Katy, had chosen the decor. Everything was pink and frilly, and a regimented line of teddy bears sat up on the bed. Sophie moved them aside and sat down with the atlas on her lap.

Katy went over to one of the mirrored double wardrobes and opened the doors. A smell of chemicals wafted out. Inside the wardrobe, instead of clothes, was a little laboratory, set up with twisted glass tubes and metal containers, and jars and bottles of coloured substances with strange labels. In the centre of the stained bench was a Bunsen burner.

'There must be something in here that can help ...' she muttered.

'Maybe ...' Sophie shivered, but she had to be brave. 'Maybe there's something in your father's study that can help us?'

'If there's any way of finding her, it'll be in one of my father's books,' Katy agreed. 'We'll have to search his study tonight. But it'd help if we had an idea of where to start looking.'

Sophie stared at the neat pinboard on Katy's wall, which held a couple of photographs, a certificate, and a postcard of Westminster Abbey.

'Hey!' she exclaimed. 'You remember those postcards

of Durham Cathedral we found? I thought they were just old postcards – but what if they had some meaning?'

'Like what?' asked Katy.

'Maybe Grandma's in Durham.' She sighed. 'But it's a big city ...'

'It's a good place to start looking, though,' Katy agreed. 'And it's only an hour from here. Though I don't know how I can explain a trip to my parents without them getting suspicious.'

'I do!' Sophie grinned as she remembered. 'Joanna lives in Durham – we can say we're going to visit her!' She grabbed her mobile. 'I'll ring my mum right now and ask her.'

'Great,' said Katy. 'And I'll think up some way of getting my parents to let us out of their sight!'

It looked like the search for her grandma wasn't over after all.

Sophie eyed the sparkling sets of knives and forks that surrounded her dinner plate. Which was she meant to use when?

She glanced up, hoping for a hint. At the head of the table, Mr Gibson ate slowly, a brooding expression on his face. Mrs Gibson delicately spread pâté on thin slices of toast. Ashton ate as if he wanted to get away from the table as soon as possible.

To Sophie's relief, Katy leaned over to her and whispered. 'Start from the outside and work your way in.'

Sophie did – and was pleasantly surprised to find that everything tasted delicious.

'This is great, Mrs Gibson,' she said, breaking the silence.

Mrs Gibson looked up and gave her a cold smile. 'How kind of you to say so,' she replied. 'Katy, dear, take your elbows off the table.'

Katy did, and Sophie copied her, blushing.

Mrs Gibson leaned forward towards them. 'So, what have you girls been doing at school lately?' she asked. Her eyes were greedily curious. 'I hear that you were set a family history project.'

Sophie suddenly found that her appetite had disappeared. She put her knife and fork down.

Ashton joined in. 'Yes, but Sophie says she didn't

find out much. She says she hasn't even met *her*.' He glanced at both his parents significantly.

Mr Gibson raised his head for the first time. Sophie thought he was going to speak, as he glanced her way – but instead he reached out for the carving knife and began slicing pieces from the joint. Sophie trembled as she watched the sharp knife slice through the pink flesh. She managed to pull her eyes away and found herself pinned between the gazes of the Gibsons.

'Do you know a Robert Lloyd?' It was Katy, speaking up next to her.

Mrs Gibson jumped and knocked over her water glass. Mr Gibson dropped the carving knife with a clatter.

'Oh, clumsy me!' Mrs Gibson dabbed at the water with a napkin, her cheeks pink.

'It's just that when I was researching our family tree,' Katy went on, 'I found that he was a second cousin of ours.'

'You must have made a mistake,' Mr Gibson said, his eyes now fixed on Katy. 'There is no Robert Lloyd in our family.'

'Well,' said Katy, opening her eyes wide and innocently. 'That's exactly what I thought!'

'Don't be thick, Katy,' Ashton said, sounding annoyed. 'We'd know about him already if he existed.'

'Right,' agreed Katy. 'Only, according to the online register of births, he's Petunia Lloyd's son.'

'Are you sure that was a reliable website you used?' Mrs Gibson said.

'She's just got it wrong, Mum,' said Ashton.

'There is no Robert Lloyd in our family,' Mr Gibson repeated. His face was emotionless, but a muscle in his jaw twitched.

Sophie noticed Katy's hand shaking as she picked up her fork, but her voice was relaxed and casual. 'I'm sure you're right. Just a bit ... odd, isn't it?' She took a mouthful of her food and, as she finished chewing it, looked up and added, 'By the way, a friend of ours – Joanna – asked if me and Sophie could go and see her tomorrow. She lives in Durham. Is that OK?'

'Good idea!' Mrs Gibson said, sounding very relieved. She glanced at Mr Gibson, who nodded. Sophie bit her cheeks to stop from grinning all across her face. Katy had outmanoeuvred her parents brilliantly! She reached down under the table and tapped her palm against Katy's in a silent high five.

After dinner, Sophie and Katy crouched at the top of the stairs, watching and listening. They heard Mrs Gibson speak on the phone below.

'Oh, hello – is that Joanna's mother?'

Katy beckoned silently to Sophie, and they tiptoed down the stairs. At the bottom, they headed towards Mr Gibson's study. As they passed the sitting-room door they could hear Mrs Gibson continuing to speak: 'They'll arrive on the 11:06 train ... Yes ... And what about these gales we've been having? Terrible, isn't it?'

Katy placed her hand on the handle of her father's study, and turned it. The door opened with hardly a squeak, and they slipped inside.

'You search the bookcase, I'll look through the desk,' Katy whispered.

Sophie nodded. She let Gally jump out of her pocket and followed him as he scampered towards the big bookshelf. She quickly scanned the titles there:

nothing about magic at all. Then she spotted a polished wooden cupboard in the corner of the room.

Sophie made her way over to it and tried the handle. It was locked. There was a small keyhole. It didn't look like a complicated lock, but she had nothing to try and pick it with.

She turned her bracelet round so that the magnet wasn't touching her skin, and brought her Source close to the lock. She hesitated, then rubbed her Source and placed it against the wood of the door.

'Forces of the Earth,' she murmured, 'let the wood soften and bend!'

The wood of the cupboard began to creak and move – warping out of shape. A few seconds later there was a click – and the lock tumbled out of the door.

Sophie quickly turned her bracelet back, and the cupboard stopped creaking. She pulled the door open. In front of her were several shelves full of books, bound in different colours of leather and cloth. She glanced at the titles.

'*How to Catch a Witch*; *Why Witches are Evil*;

Witches and their Malignant Plots Through the Ages ...' she read in horror. 'Wow, Gally, someone really doesn't like us!'

Gally hopped off her shoulder and scampered along the bookshelf. He tugged a book from its place. It was a slim volume covered in black leather, with a gold title stamped into the cover. Sophie took it from him.

'*Demagicking*,' she read. She put the book down hurriedly, remembering the live books in the secret library. What if it hurt her own magic when she touched it?

'Katy! I think Gally might have found something,' she said, her eyes still fixed on the book. She reached out and opened the cover, using just her fingertips. Nothing felt different, and she decided the book probably wasn't going to harm her.

There was a list of contents. Sophie scanned it, and let out a yelp of delight as she saw, right at the bottom, a chapter headed 'Remagicking'. Remembering where she was, she turned and looked nervously at the door, hoping no one had heard her.

Katy looked up from the desk. Sophie took one look at her face and knew she had found something important. She hurried over and looked down at the huge scroll that Katy had unrolled across the desk. It was covered in names written in Gothic script. The names at the top had faded with time. At the bottom, the names were fresh and black. Across the top, in gold lettering, were the words 'Gibson Family Tree'.

Katy pointed to a place at the bottom of the family tree. 'I'm sure a name's been rubbed out here,' she said. 'Look – you can see the shadow where it used to be.'

'Not just one name,' Sophie said breathlessly. 'Two – look.'

'You're right! It looks as if Petunia Lloyd's child was married, and then he and his wife were both erased from the family tree!' She shook her head. 'Amazing.'

She pulled open a desk drawer and lifted out a big photograph album. Sophie watched as she scanned pages full of pictures of people with the Gibson green eyes and black hair.

'You see, here's Aunt Petunia, and the twins ...' Katy shook her head. 'I know everyone here – so where's Robert Lloyd? Why aren't there any photos of him?'

She moved to close the album – but as she did so, Sophie spotted a peeling corner.

'Look!' she exclaimed. 'I think these two pages have been stuck together!

Katy slid her nail in between the pages and got them open. A photograph fell out.

Sophie picked it up. She frowned at the picture: a bride and a groom on their wedding day, both smiling happily as they hugged each other. There was something very familiar about the woman's face. Sophie frowned. Then it hit her – the bride was Angelica.

They stared at each other in shocked silence.

'But I don't understand . . . ' Katy began. 'What's she doing in my family album? She's a witch!'

She took the photo from Sophie and turned it over.

'There's something written on the back here,' she said. She brought it closer to the lamp, and read aloud: 'Robert Lloyd. But then . . . look.' She showed Sophie the writing, and that the name 'Robert Lloyd' had a line through it.

Katy stared at Sophie with her mouth open. 'So Angelica was married to Robert Lloyd,' she said softly. 'Sophie, this explains everything. Don't you see? Angelica's a witch ... and Robert Lloyd was a witch hunter. No wonder they erased him from the family tree!'

SEVENTEEN

Sophie glanced at the door. They had to move fast – but she could hardly tear herself away from the photograph. A witch married to a witch hunter!

'It's so sad,' she said, looking back at the photo. Angelica looked so happy in it, and so did Robert – a tall, red-headed young man with spectacles. It was hard to imagine that the wild-eyed Angelica they had met was the same person as this calm, smiling woman. 'Just because he married a witch, they cut him out of the family.'

Katy nodded. 'Poor Robert!'

Sophie couldn't help wondering if Katy's parents would cut her out of the family as well, if they ever discovered she was best friends with a witch. *Poor Katy*, she thought.

'I don't understand,' she said aloud. 'How does Angelica fit into all this?'

'We'll have to find out,' Katy nodded. 'But not now – my father could come in any minute.

'Quick, let's look at this book you've found.' She held out her hand and Sophie passed her the book.

Katy opened it at the chapter on remagicking.

'Here we are,' she said. 'The ingredients you need to remagick a witch: Dodo feathers, carbonised mandrake root, ground up witch Sources . . .'

'How on earth are we going to get all that?' Sophie asked.

'They're rare ingredients,' Katy agreed, 'but I think my parents might have some.' She shut the book. 'I won't look now, though. We've been here long enough – we'd better go before we get caught.' She glanced round the room and handed the book to

Sophie. 'Quick, we need to make everything look like it was when we came in!'

Sophie shut the cupboard and placed her Source on the wood again, so it warped back into shape. Katy tidied the desk and switched off the lamp.

Sophie walked back to the door, giving the room a quick glance over her shoulder to make sure it looked OK. Katy's hand was on the door handle when it opened so suddenly that she stumbled backwards, bumping into Sophie and sending her sprawling across the desk.

Mr Gibson loomed in the doorway.

Sophie gasped and put the book behind her back. She felt Gally scamper from the desk onto her clothes and up between her T-shirt and jumper.

Mr Gibson's his eyes blazed in anger. 'What are you doing in here?' he roared. 'You know this office is out of bounds!'

'I – we – we – were just looking for a pen to do our homework,' Katy gabbled, edging towards the door. 'I'm really sorry, Dad. We won't do it again!'

Sophie felt behind her with one hand and picked a

pen up from the desk. With the book still hidden behind her back, she showed Mr Gibson the pen, and joined in Katy's apologies.

Mr Gibson scowled at them. 'Well, make sure you never do it again! If you want a pen, ask your mother.'

'Yes, Dad. Sorry!'

Sophie, her heart hammering, sidled out of the door, Katy following her. As soon as they got into the corridor, Sophie stuffed the book up her jumper, feeling Gally take it from her, and they ran upstairs without daring to look back.

'Wow,' said Sophie, gazing up at Durham Cathedral. The towers were bathed in golden light and the sun shone on the rose window. 'It's beautiful!'

'It is!' Katy agreed.

Sophie glanced at her watch. It was almost 11.30a.m., and they'd told Joanna that their train had been delayed until 1.15p.m. 'Come on,' Sophie said. 'We've got less than two hours to find my grandma.'

Katy glanced up and down the path, then took a silver chain from round her neck. 'We might as well try this first, just in case,' she murmured. She pulled out the pendant on the end of the chain and Sophie recognised it at once. It was a Witch Hunter's Bloodhound.

'Is that Ashton's?' she asked.

'No, but he has one. It will point us to a witch if there's one near,' Katy said. She dangled the pendant, letting it twirl back and forth. 'Of course, because your Grandma's been demagicked it probably won't work.'

Katy gasped as the pendant shot towards Sophie, jerking the chain taut round her neck. She threw up her arms to defend herself, and the pendant scratched her across the back of her hand. A high-pitched noise, just like the one she'd heard when she first opened *Magic Most Dark,* pierced Sophie's ears. The end of the pendant wasn't sharp but Sophie saw the blood oozing from a cut.

'Oh, Sophie! Are you OK?' Katy closed the pendant hurriedly. 'I'm so sorry. I didn't think!'

'I'm fine,' Sophie laughed, though she felt a little shaken. She sucked at the scratch on her hand, which stung.

'Once we've done the remagicking ritual we can try again,' Katy told her. 'But you'll have to turn your bracelet round first!'

Sophie flipped her friendship bracelet so the magnet was touching her then sat down on the grass and opened her bag. 'You can come out now, Gally – go and stretch your legs,' she told the squirrel. Gally ran out, sniffed round and, with a happy whisk of his black tail, darted straight up the nearest tree.

Katy, who was sitting next to her, carefully lifted a Thermos out of her bag.

'This is it,' she announced, unscrewing the top and showing Sophie the grey powder inside. 'It will remagick any demagicked witch in the area, and the effects will last until the moon is up.'

'Wow.' There was so much about witch hunter magic that Sophie didn't know.

'I hope I've got it right! It's the most complicated formula I've ever made.'

'It certainly smells complicated!' Sophie said, wrinkling her nose.

'Mmm, that's the Dodo feathers.' Katy said. 'I

managed to get everything from my parents' supply cupboard – except for a pig's bladder.'

'Ew!' Sophie made a face.

'That's what I thought,' Katy agreed. She took a limp balloon and a funnel out of her bag. 'I thought a balloon might do just as well anyway – it's for the container.'

She passed the balloon and the funnel to Sophie. 'If you hold the funnel into the neck of the balloon, I'll pour the powder in.'

Sophie took another look at the scratch. It had stopped bleeding. She held open the balloon as Katy poured in the powder. The balloon inflated as the powder entered it and, when the last grains had gone in, Sophie tied a knot in the neck. She looked at Katy for instructions.

'Now we've got to drop it on the ground, so that it bursts,' Katy told her. She took the balloon from Sophie and carried it over to the path.

'Well, here goes!' They hugged each other quickly for luck, then Katy dropped the balloon. It burst with a bang that made Sophie jump. The grey powder scattered everywhere, was caught by the breeze and carried away; soon they couldn't see it at all.

Sophie broke the silence. 'I don't feel any different,' she said. 'But then I don't need remagicking.'

Katy shook her head. 'It won't affect you.' She gazed into the air, as if she could still see the dust. 'We just have to hope that your grandma's nearby and that the formula worked.' She took the pendant from round her neck, unfolded it and let it dangle. The chain twisted and turned as the needle spun itself round and round. It settled unnaturally quickly – pointing towards the cathedral.

'It's found a witch!' Katy said, looking pale but excited. 'Come on – let's follow it.'

Sophie really hoped that they would find her grandma. But she didn't know if her grandma would mind being found by witch-hunter methods.

Sophie raced into the cathedral after Katy. Their feet echoed in the quiet. An old lady in the pews frowned at them and put a finger to her lips.

'Sorry,' Sophie whispered breathlessly. The bar

pendant twirled and pointed to the left. Katy followed it. Sophie went after her. The needle, tugging at its silver chain, led them up the nave. Sophie glanced up, awed by the enormous height and the stone angels that loomed above them. At the altar, the needle led them into a side chapel.

'It's pulling really hard,' Katy gasped. 'There must be a witch very close by—' She broke off as the needle dragged her towards a wooden door marked PRIVATE. Sophie glanced round. No one was watching, so she turned the handle. It opened onto a stone staircase, leading down. The needle tipped, pointing down the stairs.

At the bottom was a large, low room supported by pillars. It was cool and damp. The needle led them in and out of the pillars and deep into the shadows, which led into another chamber. More steps led down. Their footsteps rang on the stone.

They passed a bright orange sign warning: DANGER – EXCAVATIONS. Another sign told them: HARD HATS MUST BE WORN AT ALL TIMES. Plastic sheets were spread everywhere.

The needle tugged Katy firmly towards some security tape that was strung across a carved doorway.

'It says "Do Not Cross" Katy said, hesitating. The next moment, the needle yanked her forward and with a squeal she was pulled through the security tape and the door. Sophie ran after her.

They were looking down some steps into a shadowy stone chamber. Old memorial stones were set into the walls and floor, and shafts of sunlight came down through cracked flagstones. As Sophie watched, a woman came into sight, pacing up and down and wringing her hands.

Sophie broke into a grin as a sunbeam lit the woman's face.

'Grandma!' she cried, and raced down the steps into her grandmother's arms.

EIGHTEEN

'Grandma, it's so good to see you!' Sophie hugged her tightly. 'We've been so worried!'

'Oh, what a lovely surprise! But how did you find me, darling? Where's your mother?' Sophie's grandma asked, returning her hug.

Sophie quickly told her what had happened. Her grandmother listened in astonishment. At the mention of *Magic Most Dark*, she started and her hand went to her mouth.

'We think Angelica must have taken it,' Sophie told her. 'Don't we, Katy?'

Her grandma's eyes darted to Katy, who was standing shyly back, and Sophie felt her tense. 'Is this your . . . the witch hunter?'

Sophie stepped towards Katy and took her hand. 'This is my best friend, Katy Gibson,' she said firmly. 'And Grandma – she's remagicked you. Your powers are back.'

'What?' her grandmother gasped. 'No – it can't be true!'

'It is,' Katy said, swallowing before she could speak again. 'Although the spell only works until moon-up, I'm afraid.'

Sophie's grandmother's eyes shone with a strange, fierce light. Sophie squeezed Katy's hand and moved in front of her, suddenly afraid that her grandmother might use her powers to hurt Katy. But her grandmother stroked the necklace of jade beads that hung round her neck and glanced round the room. Sophie saw her walk over to a weed, growing yellow and straggly through a crack in the stone towards a shaft of light. Her grandmother whispered a few words under her breath and touched the weed. Sophie gasped as the plant exploded into a flourishing bush, pushing the flagstones around it up as its roots grew. It blossomed with white flowers and a sweet smell filled the room.

'Beautiful,' Sophie's grandmother murmured, looking at the bush in delight. She turned to Katy. 'Thank you, my dear. You've given me back myself – even if for only a few hours.' Her voice was warm, and Katy blushed again, but this time she was smiling. 'I will never forget this.'

Grandma turned back to Sophie. 'I cannot believe the danger you have been through to reach me. I feel terrible. I should have protected you better.' She clasped her hands. '*Magic Most Dark* is a perilous book; an evil book.'

'So why doesn't someone destroy it?' Sophie asked. 'Maybe that's what Angelica is doing.'

'It can't be destroyed,' her grandma told her. 'But we thought it would be safe, where we hid it.'

'We?' said Katy and Sophie at the same moment.

Sophie added: '*You* hid it, Grandma?'

'Myself and another witch.' Her grandmother

looked away from Sophie so she couldn't see her face. 'We thought a blank book would be overlooked in a human library. But then you found it.' She looked at Sophie. 'Did you hear a noise as you opened it?'

'Yes!' Sophie exclaimed. 'A sharp, piercing noise.'

Her grandmother nodded. 'That was an alarm spell, set to warn us if a witch opened the book. Once it had been found, we had to hide it even more securely. Then the witch I was working with put a curse on the library so that it became a maze – making it even more difficult to find.'

'But wait,' Sophie said, feeling her heart start to beat fast. 'The postcard in the book. It was of Durham Cathedral, just like the one that was signed with an F. Is that F for ... Franklin?'

Her grandma hesitated for a moment before nodding again. 'Yes ... Your father was the other witch.'

'So he *was* there!' Sophie's heart raced and she could feel the tears prickling her eyes. Katy took hold of her hand.

'He sent me the postcard when he heard the alarm. The same spell that kept the evil book blank also kept it hidden from the witch who created it – but when you picked it up, it started to call to its creator. I had to hide because I knew that the creator would try to hurt me using the book. Franklin let me know this would be a safe place to hide.'

Sophie hung her head. 'He came to Turlingham and he didn't even want to see me and Mum.' She rubbed the back of her hand across her eyes.

'Oh, my dear,' said her grandmother gently, 'be sure that he *did* want to.' She laid a hand on Sophie's shoulder. 'But it is hasn't been simple.'

Sophie nodded. It was hard, but she wanted to trust her father.

'So, tell me again, who do you think has taken it?' her grandmother asked.

'Her name is Angelica.' She hastily explained about the air vent and the footprints.

'Angelica ...' Her grandmother frowned. 'I don't recognise the name. But if she went to such trouble to find the book, even risking being trapped in the library maze for ever, she must have evil intentions.'

Katy and Sophie swapped a glance. So Angelica had

been in the library of her own free will – Franklin hadn't trapped her there. Sophie sighed with relief.

Grandma looked up sharply. 'Are you sure this Angelica is not a witch hunter? Many of the spells in that book can be used to catch and kill witches.'

'They can be used against witch hunters, too,' Katy spoke up.

'I'm sure she's a witch,' said Sophie. 'She was married to a witch hunter, Katy's second cousin – Robert Lloyd.'

Her grandmother gasped and a look of shock came over her face.

'What's the matter?' Sophie asked, frightened at her grandmother's expression.

'How do you know this? Are you sure?' Her grandmother grabbed Sophie's wrist, so tight that it hurt.

Sophie panicked. Her grandma's eyes were wild. 'Yes! I'm certain!'

'Can you describe her? Quick – you must tell me!' She shook Sophie.

Katy, looking as frightened as Sophie felt, reached

out to try and break her grip on Sophie's wrist. Sophie's grandmother pushed her aside.

'Well, s-she was a-about my mother's age,' Sophie stammered, 'and she had long, curly brown hair, and strange clothes – and her familiar was a cat. Named Mincing.'

As she spoke, she heard a *meow* from the steps behind her. She turned round – and saw Mincing standing on the steps. Behind her was a shadow. As the shadow moved forward, Sophie gasped: 'Angelica!'

Her grandmother dropped Sophie's wrist. 'No . . .' she said, her eyes fixed on Angelica.

Angelica brought something out from behind her back. It was *Magic Most Dark*. The witch's eyes flared with cold anger as she moved forward, slowly flicking through the pages of the book.

'How did you get that out of the library?' Sophie demanded.

Angelica laughed. 'It wasn't hard. Franklin's spells are easy to break when you know how. And I've had years of practice.' She held Sophie's grandmother's gaze for a moment.

'You know my father that well?' Sophie said, shocked.

'We all know each other very well,' her grandma said, and Sophie was startled by the sadness in her voice. 'Although the name is new.'

'Well, I had to change my name, once the witch community had ostracised me!' Angelica hissed. Her hard gaze softened as she glanced between Sophie and Katy. 'It's difficult, isn't it, when a witch and a witch hunter care about each other?'

Sophie and Katy swapped a look. Angelica was right about that.

'I loved Robert so much,' Angelica said softly, as if to herself. 'When everyone we knew threw us out, we had no one but each other. We created this book, full of dark magic, so that we could protect ourselves against any witch or witch hunter who tried to separate us. Now he's gone. I don't know if he is alive or dead.' Sophie saw tears glittering in her eyes, and Mincing wound herself round her ankles, as if to comfort her. 'I've been so alone ... so lonely, for so long.' She sighed, and gave them a sudden, chillingly brilliant smile. 'I don't think I'm quite sane any more, do you?'

Sophie looked desperately at her grandmother. But her grandmother was staring at Angelica as if she were about to burst into tears.

'Don't look at *her* for help,' Angelica said scornfully, following Sophie's gaze. 'She's the evil one, don't you see?'

Angelica tossed the book up into the air. It hovered there, above her hand, and the pages flicked over like licking tongues of fire before settling at a particular spell. Sophie gasped and backed away. The jewelled eyes of Angelica's jade hairslide flashed.

Reading from the book as it hovered before her, Angelica shouted out some strange words. In her hand, a crystal orb appeared. It was full of glowing red sparks, and made a high buzzing noise as if there were mosquitoes trapped inside.

'What is that?' Katy hissed to Sophie.

'I don't know – nothing good.' Sophie's voice rose to a scream as Angelica raised the orb – and flung it straight at her grandmother. 'Look out! Grandma!'

Grandma grabbed a sheet of corrugated iron and just managed to block the orb before it hit her. The orb disappeared with a hiss-like steam as it hit the iron, leaving a blazing hole in the metal. Sophie's grandmother flung the remains of the sheet away.

'Get behind me, girls.' She touched her necklace and raised her arms in a powerful, sweeping gesture, just as Angelica flung another orb at her. A shield of water appeared between Sophie's grandmother's outstretched hands, and the orb rebounded from it and hit a wall, bursting in a shower of sparks.

'Stop this, please!' Sophie's grandmother cried to Angelica. 'Your powers could be used for good!'

Angelica advanced, laughing as another orb formed in her hand. 'Good and evil – such outdated concepts!' she said. 'They are all in the eye of the beholder, don't you think?'

'Killing people is evil!' Sophie screamed at her. The orb flew towards them and her grandmother drew a shield of flames between them. The orb vaporised as it hit the shield, showering sparks everywhere.

'Sophie, Katy, do you have some kind of rope? A

hairband? Anything like that?' Sophie's grandmother gasped under her breath as Angelica began to chant again.

Sophie reached for her friendship bracelet, then hesitated for a second before undoing it. She tore the magnet out and threw it away.

'Powers of earth and darkness, powers of the stone and the stars, hear me!' Angelica chanted, gazing into the book.

'Repeat after me, Sophie,' her grandmother ordered. 'Water, wind, fire and earth, twist your strength into this bond.'

Sophie repeated the spell, and twisted the friendship bracelet between her fingers, allowing her Source to touch it. The charms shimmered.

Angelica looked up, a fearsome grin on her face. She held a bigger orb this time, and it was black, with a spinning red tornado at the heart of it.

'When she attacks, throw the bracelet at her,' Sophie's grandmother commanded.

Angelica raised the orb and hurled it at them. It screamed as it cut through the air. Sophie swung the friendship bracelet like a lasso and flung it at Angelica.

The bracelet snaked through the air, growing as it did so. Leaves sprouted from it, and suddenly it was a thick, rope-like vine. It sliced through the orb, which popped like a balloon and hit Angelica. It coiled itself round her, binding her tightly to the nearest pillar. Angelica shrieked with rage as the book fell to the floor with a flutter of pages.

Katy ran to pick up the book but, as she touched it, flames shot out of the cover and she snatched her hand back with a gasp of pain. The flames sank back into the cover, leaving the book unharmed.

Angelica laughed. 'No one can touch it now except me!'

'We'll get it another day,' panted Sophie's grandmother. 'Come on, girls, we have to go.'

Sophie followed her grandmother towards the exit. Angelica's eyes were hot with hatred. As they reached the arch, Sophie's grandmother turned back to Angelica. In a gentle, almost pleading voice she said, 'The spell will not last long. You'll be free soon.'

She turned and hurried out of the room. Sophie was startled to see a tear roll down her cheek.

'Why has Angelica upset you so much, Grandma?'

But her grandmother quickly brushed the tear away. 'Call your mother,' she told Sophie. 'I think it's time for us to go home.'

NINETEEN

Sophie pulled aside her bedroom curtains and looked out. In the school courtyard, her year were milling round, laughing and chatting. All of them were dressed in masks and costumes. She sighed. It felt odd to be back home, back in Turlingham, after so much had happened. There was a new scar on her hand from the scratch the Witch Hunter's Bloodhound gave her, so she would never forget. But she didn't want to think about Angelica any more, or the book of dark magic. And she definitely didn't want to think about her dad ... would he ever come back to Turlingham again? Why hadn't he come to see them? She knew Grandma was right, and there were dangers in the way ... but she just wished he had managed it, somehow.

No, she wasn't going to think of that – tonight was all about having fun.

'Time to go, Gally!' she said, letting the curtains drop and running to the mirror for one last look at her costume. 'What do you think?' she added to the squirrel, pulling on her mask. She stroked her long whiskers and did her best squirrel impersonation.

Gally put his head on one side doubtfully. Sophie laughed.

'Oh, come on! I'm quite proud of it – especially the tail.' She smoothed her long, silky black tail, which she'd made out of a feather boa. The rest of her costume was black leggings and a black T-shirt.

'I think I look like your twin,' she teased Gally, scooping him up and putting him in her bag. She hurried downstairs. Her mother was waiting for her at the bottom.

'You look nice, Sophie,' she said.

'Thanks, Mum. And thanks for letting me go tonight.'

'Well, I think you've learned your lesson after being grounded for most of half term. I hope you have, anyway,' she added, sternly but with a smile. 'No matter how worried you were about your grandma, you should never have lied to me. You could have got yourself in real danger, rushing off to Durham to meet her like that.'

Sophie nodded, hanging her head. There was no way she could tell her mum the whole truth, even now.

She went outside to where her friends were waiting for her.

'Sophie!' A girl dressed as the Statue of Liberty broke away from the crowd, waving to her. Sophie squealed as she recognised Erin, and ran to hug her.

'You look amazing!' they said at the same moment, then laughed.

'I dyed a sheet bluey-grey, and the crown's a paper plate,' Erin said proudly.

'Hi, Sophie.' Kaz came forward wearing a sparkly blue dress under a black cape. Sophie thought she sounded a little more distant than usual, but she smiled in her usual friendly way.

'What are you?' Sophie asked her.

'A witch! Hang on, you need the mask for the full look,' Kaz said, putting it on. Sophie stifled a grin as she saw it had green skin, a big nose, a pointy chin and a wart.

'Very ... realistic,' she said.

'Hi, guys,' Sophie turned. It was Katy's voice – but it came from a pretty elf who was walking towards them, dressed in a long, flowing robe straight out of Elfin Warriors.

'Oh, Katy, what a beautiful mask!' Lauren exclaimed. Lauren was dressed as Queen Elizabeth I, complete with the ruff round her neck and orb and sceptre.

'Did you honestly make that?' Erin said.

'Yeah,' Katy pulled her mask up, smiling. 'I didn't have anything else to do after Sophie went home.'

Sophie pulled her to one side. 'You have to show Callum your mask!' she said under her breath. 'He'll love it.' She beamed at her friend, delighted. Perhaps tonight would finally be the time for Callum and Katy to get together.

'Oh,' she said, remembering, 'and you can have your friendship bracelet back now, Katy!' She slipped the bracelet into Katy's hand.

'Thanks!' Katy said, taking it. 'I'm sorry you had to lose yours.'

'Me too ... but there was no other way.'

'What did you want to borrow it for, anyway?' Katy asked as she tied the bracelet round her wrist.

'I just made an ... addition,' said Sophie, smiling. 'It might come in useful one day.' *Although I hope it never has to*, she thought.

'Ready, kids?' called Mr McGowan, waving a stick with bells on in the air.

'What *is* he wearing?' Sophie's mouth fell open as she stared at his white clothes, and the bells and ribbons tied round his knees and arms.

'Shhh! It's a morris-dancing outfit,' Katy whispered. They exchanged a glance and doubled over with silent laughter.

'Off we go to the pagan festival! With a hey nonny no,' Mr McGowan said, beaming. He turned and marched off down the road, jingling as he went. Sophie and the rest of the Year 9s followed him, giggling.

Sophie squeezed through the crowds. She'd never seen Turlingham village so full of people. Many of the shops were open, with stalls for apple bobbing, local handicrafts and foods. Children whooped and ran screaming here and there, clutching sparklers and candyfloss.

'This is great!' Katy said, looking round, her eyes shining.

'Oh, look!' yelped Erin. 'The Seagull Café has got a special festival ice cream. Let's get some!' She hurried over to the shop with the others behind her.

Sophie was about to follow when Katy held her back. 'Did your grandma tell you anything else about your dad?' Katy asked her.

Sophie shook her head sadly. 'I've asked and asked – but nothing.'

'I'm sorry,' Katy said.

Sophie forced a smile. 'Don't be! We're here to have fun, aren't we?' She looked round and her eyes fell on a stall overflowing with film memorabilia.

'I am! It's so cool being in disguise,' Katy said. She added. 'There's Oliver – shall we go and say hi?'

'You go on, I just want to stop and look at this stall,' Sophie told her. Katy ran ahead while Sophie paused and looked at the posters that were spread out. She reached for a little model of a werewolf – and her hand bumped into a boy's hand as he reached for the same thing.

Sophie looked up, and gulped as she found herself looking into the hairy, snarling face of an Alsatian. A second later she realised it was a mask – of course. The boy was in costume.

'Sorry,' she said, drawing her hand back.

'No, you have it,' the boy said. 'I've got one like this at home already.' He looked her up and down. 'Nice squirrel outfit, by the way. I like the tail. Very bushy.'

'Thanks!' Sophie was glad her mask covered her blush. 'Nice ... dog outfit.'

'You're welcome,' the boy said. He leaned back and

surveyed her. 'Hang on,' he said, with a smile in his voice, 'if you're a squirrel I should be chasing you, shouldn't I?'

Sophie's eyes sparkled with mischief.

She turned and sprinted away, weaving in and out of the crowd. She went on her hands and knees under a stall selling old books, and came up, glancing round. The boy was nowhere in sight, so she made to run off down the street – but someone grabbed her by the shoulder and spun her round.

'Gotcha!'

Sophie laughed, breathlessly, as the boy in the dog costume held her in his arms.

'You're a – pretty – fast – dog!' she said.

The boy didn't reply, but leaned in towards her. Sophie's eyes widened, and her heart speeded up. For a fleeting instant, she thought he was about to kiss her.

'Thanks. But I'm not a dog,' he said in a low voice. 'I'm a werewolf, like the one in *Full Moon*.'

'*Full Moon?*' Sophie said as a sudden memory came into her head.

'Yes – it's my favourite movie.'

Sophie quickly pulled out of his grasp.

Taken by surprise, he let her go. 'What's the matter?' he asked.

Behind her, Erin's voice called: 'Sophie! *There* you are! Come and look at this awesome charm stall!'

'Sophie?' said the boy, sounding shocked.

Ashton! Sophie turned and raced towards Erin without a backward glance. *That did not just happen!* she told herself. She blushed at the thought of how close they'd come to kissing. *Get a grip, Sophie – that was* Ashton Gibson!

Sophie was looking at the bath bombs when she felt someone tug her arm.

'Sophie,' Katy said, 'I haven't found Callum. Will you come with me to look for him, please?'

'Of course! He's got to see your elf mask.' Sophie left the stall and went with Katy. They walked arm in arm through the crowd, scanning for Callum.

'Maybe he's over in that park,' Sophie said, pointing towards a small green area where some benches stood.

As they walked towards the benches, Sophie saw

that there were two people sitting on one of them. She hesitated, but Katy went on a few steps before stopping still.

'That's Callum,' she said, under her breath.

Callum had his mask pushed back over his head. He was wearing armour, like the hero in Elfin Warriors. As they watched, they heard him speak.

'I *really* like you,' he said nervously. 'A lot.'

Sophie's heart sank like a stone. The girl turned towards them, and Sophie saw that she was wearing a green witch's mask. It was Kaz.

Katy put a hand to her mouth.

'Oh, Katy,' Sophie murmured.

Katy turned round. Sophie saw tears gleaming in her eyes as she raced off into the crowd.

'Katy!' Sophie ran after her, but found her way blocked by a troupe of morris dancers.

'There you are, Sophie!' Mr McGowan said, taking her arm. 'It's time for the parade. This is the Earl of Turlingham—'

'How do you do?' enquired a tall, posh-voiced morris dancer.

'. . . who will take you onto the family float.'

'It's your right,' said the earl, 'as one of the family!'

'Oh – but – but I . . .' Sophie gasped. She tried to look round them to find Katy, but she had disappeared.

'Don't worry, my dear. Quite natural to be shy,' the earl told her, taking her arm and steering her through the crowd. 'All you have to do is smile and wave.'

Sophie found herself helped onto the Turlingham float by smiling people she had never seen before. The float was a scale model of Turlingham itself: the school looming over the village, winding streets leading down to the harbour. The cliffs even had models of seagulls on wires stuck into them. Sophie wobbled as she tried not to tread on them.

She steadied herself on the model of the clock tower and stared along the parade, looking for Katy among the brightly coloured floats. There were people dressed as witches and knights and dragons . . . but no elves.

'So you're a relative!' the earl said, clambering up beside her. 'How interesting—'

To Sophie's great relief, the marching band struck

up, drowning him out. The float set off jerkily. The crowds waved and cheered. Sophie, blushing furiously and wishing she was anywhere else, hung onto the float with one hand and waved back with the other. She scanned the crowd as fireworks began to go off across the sky, lighting the clock tower in different colours. Callum and Katy were nowhere to be seen.

Then there was a sudden flash of blinding light and a deafening bang. Sophie felt as if she was being sucked through the air, and her stomach went into free fall. As her vision cleared, and her head stopped spinning, she gasped.

She wasn't on the float any longer. She was in a small stone room. Above her she could see massive gears, and the face of a clock from behind. To both sides were arched openings, through which the cold wind blew.

Where on earth was she? And what kind of magic had brought her here?

TWENTY

Sophie raced to one of the windows and looked out. She was in the clock tower. Down in the street she could see the crowds and the float where she had been standing until a second ago. Fireworks whistled up above her head and burst in showers of light. She heard voices floating up to her:

'Amazing!'

'Just disappeared!'

'Great trick!'

A hand grabbed her shoulder and jerked her away

from the window. Sophie stumbled back. A malicious *meow* came from near her feet and as her eyes got used to the shadows she realised she was looking into Angelica's face.

'Join me,' hissed Angelica. She was gripping the book of dark magic so hard that her knuckles were white.

Sophie shook her head, too frightened and confused to speak. Outside the fireworks snapped and crackled, throwing coloured light across Angelica's face.

'But why not, dear Sophie?' Angelica demanded. Mincing echoed her with a sharp mew. 'We could be so strong together. This book contains the most powerful witch and witch hunter magic that I and my darling Robert could collect. It was made by two, and if two people use it, two people who are close, through love or blood, the magic is even stronger.' Her voice dropped, wheedling. 'You've seen how powerful I am alone. Imagine the power we could have together!'

'I don't want to join you!' Sophie sobbed, backing away. 'And we're not close!'

'Exactly what my poor deluded brother said, when

I offered him this extraordinary chance,' Angelica said thoughtfully. 'Ah, well. We can do it the hard way.'

Sophie felt something prod into her back and turned round to see she had backed against a large metal ring in the wall. She was trapped. Her eyes went to the door opposite her but, before she could make a break for it, Angelica leapt towards her and Sophie saw the flash of metal in her hands. The next moment Angelica had wrapped a chain round Sophie's hands and fastened the chain to the ring. Sophie tugged at the chain, but it was no good.

Angelica turned away from her, with a swirl of her long skirts. 'She will join me,' she muttered, and Sophie realised she was talking to herself. 'She will, even if I have to make her!'

'But why *me*?' Sophie said pleadingly, as she struggled with the chain,

'I won't let my wretched brother win!' Angelica went on, her voice rising to a harsh scream. She shook her head violently, then turned to Sophie. 'If he won't recognise the importance of family and join me, perhaps his daughter will.'

Sophie felt herself turn white. Family? Daughter? That meant Angelica was . . .

'Of course,' she murmured. She raised her voice. 'You're Gertrude!'

Mincing gave a terrible yowl and Angelica whipped round, fixing Sophie with a savage glare. 'Never use that name again!' she spat. 'I left it behind, a long time ago . . . with the rest of my past.'

Sophie trembled. *This madwoman is my aunt!*

The door banged open behind Angelica. Sophie looked up. Katy was standing in the doorway, breathing hard.

'Sophie!' she gasped.

'Katy! You came to save me!' Sophie cried.

Angelica laughed scornfully. 'Come to save you? I don't think so. Why, this good little witch hunter was the one who led me to you.'

'I don't believe you,' Sophie shouted.

At the same moment Katy said: 'That's a lie!'

'Come on, Sophie, consider the evidence,' Angelica said, casually leafing through the book of dark magic. 'There's a scar on your hand, isn't there? From the

Witch Hunter's Bloodhound? I heard the alarm and it led me straight to you in Durham.'

'That was an accident,' Katy said. She turned to Sophie. 'Sophie, you don't believe her, do you?'

Sophie glanced at her hand, and the long silvery scratch. She shook her head. 'No, I don't,' she said firmly. She looked up at Angelica and added, 'Witches and witch hunters can trust each other. You of all people should know that!'

'Trust!' Angelica spat. 'No one can be trusted. Neither witches nor witch hunters. Except me, of course.' She reached out a hand to Sophie. 'Come and join me, and soon all witches and witch hunters will be destroyed for ever.'

Sophie stared back. 'I'll think about it,' she said, her heart beating fast. 'Give me a moment.'

Behind her, Katy took a sharp intake of breath.

'You have ten seconds!' Angelica said, and paced to the window. As soon as her back was turned, Sophie spat onto the chains that bound her hands.

'Forces of the Earth,' she muttered, 'rust this chain!'

The water in her spit bubbled and red rust

appeared on the chain. It crumbled through and the remains of the chain fell to the ground with a clatter. Sophie ran towards Katy as Angelica spun round.

'Trickster!' Angelica screamed. She raised her hand, and the book flew up into the air. She muttered some words and, before Sophie and Katy could reach the door, a wall of flame leapt in front of them, blocking their escape. They flinched back from it.

Angelica chanted fiercely, her eyes on the page.

Sophie snatched a hair from her head and held it up. 'Forces of the Earth, make this hair strong!' she shouted. The hair grew into a shining blade. Angelica simply laughed and waved her hand. A gale-force wind roared through the small stone room, and Sophie staggered as the hair blade was torn from her hands and disappeared in a flash of light.

There was already an orb in Angelica's hands.

'You can't stop me,' she sneered. 'My magic is dark – more powerful than yours.'

Sophie ducked as the orb flew towards her. She called on the Forces of the Earth and brought up a shield of wind to blow the orbs away. The orbs bounced off it, but Sophie staggered as the energy was sucked from her. Angelica was too strong. They had to think of something – fast.

She glanced behind her. Katy was crouching on the ground, searching through pillboxes and vials as she mixed liquids and shimmering powders.

'It's a demagicking formula,' she told Sophie. 'If I can remember how to do it, I can cast it onto her!'

Sophie gasped as the orbs smashed into her shield. She dodged here and there, trying to avoid the orbs. She glanced behind her: Katy was shaking a test tube with a worried look. Sophie didn't know if she wanted to see a demagicking, she imagined the process would be brutal.

'It's not working,' Katy called back. 'I think there's an ingredient I don't have!'

Angelica laughed. 'You're a fool to listen to a witch hunter's lies!'

With a final effort, Sophie sent the shield of wind careering towards her. Angelica ducked, and Sophie grabbed Katy's hand and they raced for the door. But, before they could reach it, a sheet of ice grew over the door, crackling as it blocked their way. Sophie spun round. The orb was already hurtling towards her. There was no way she could stop it in time. She closed her eyes and prepared herself for its impact.

But the blow didn't come. She opened her eyes – and saw Katy, lying on the floor – her eyes open but unseeing, her face white. She wasn't breathing.

TWENTY-ONE

'Katy!' Sophie screamed. She dropped to the floor next to her friend. Katy was wearing her friendship bracelet. Frantically she looked to see if the addition was still there ...

Angelica moved towards Sophie, stretching out a hand to her, an orb in the other hand.

'Join me!' she begged once more. 'Please ... I don't want to hurt you. But I will.'

The door burst open, and a man in a long, dark coat came striding through it.

Sophie gasped and looked up as the man shouted: 'Gertrude!'

The man raised his hands and a whirlwind sucked the book out of Angelica's reach. Angelica hissed and tried to fling the orb at him, but the whirlwind caught it and dashed it against the wall. The twin brother and sister faced each other. They were the same height and had the same fierce eyes.

He looked older than she remembered, with more grey hairs and a grizzled beard, but Sophie knew him instantly. It was her father, Franklin Poulter.

Franklin caught Angelica's arms and restrained her. 'How could you do this?' he demanded.

Angelica twisted out of his grip, scratching at his face. Franklin leapt back and reached into his coat. He pulled out a gold, engraved pocket watch and held it tightly in his palm.

As her father muttered a few words and a whirlwind started up from the floor and rose into the air, Sophie realised that the watch was her father's Source. The whirlwind got faster and faster and Angelica backed away from it in fear. It closed in on her, trapping her within it and spinning her round and round.

'Help me!' she screamed.

'Dad!' shouted Sophie. 'You're hurting her!'

But Sophie's dad didn't respond.

'Let me go!' Angelica screamed again.

'Dad! Please!' Sophie shouted again. She'd seen enough pain inflicted for one night. She didn't want to see anyone else get hurt. Least of all her own aunt.

Franklin looked from his daughter to his sister and his face softened. 'You must promise to never, ever come back,' Franklin told her.

'Yes! I promise. Anything you say, just make it stop!'

He gestured towards the whirlwind, and it died down. Angelica toppled dizzily out of it and fell to the floor. She scrambled up, gave one last furious look at Sophie's father, and made for the door. Mincing scurried after her. At the door, Angelica paused and glanced back towards Sophie, a look of terrible sorrow and loneliness on her face. Then she turned and was gone, her footsteps dying away as she ran down the stairs, until there was silence.

Sophie looked down at her friend, cradled in her arms. 'Katy! Wake up!'

Katy moaned, and opened her eyes.

'Katy!' Sophie exclaimed. 'Are you OK?'

'Y-yes.' Katy pulled herself into a sitting position. 'But *how*, Sophie? I was hit with the full force of her magic!' She put a hand to her head. 'I shouldn't be alive!'

Sophie smiled. 'Look at your friendship bracelet.'

Katy looked at her bracelet and gasped. 'Sophie! You've worked in your gold earrings. They protected me – but they were your favourites!'

Sophie laughed. 'Come on, Katy – I'd give up all my earrings for the sake of my best friend.'

'Oh, Sophie!' Katy flung her arms round her. She pulled back, looking into Sophie's face. 'I promise I didn't know the cut on your hand would lead Angelica to you. I would never betray you. I promise I would never—'

Sophie interrupted her with a warm smile. 'I know.' They hugged each other tightly.

Over Katy's shoulder, Sophie saw someone else smiling at her from the door – her father.

'I can't believe how much you've grown,' Franklin Poulter said, stopping once again to look at Sophie. Around them, the crowd laughed and talked as they made their way through the winding village streets towards the parade. Katy walked a little way behind, Sophie guessed she was trying to give her some space to talk with her dad.

Sophie laughed in embarrassment as he smiled at her.

'Dad, I'm glad you're back,' she said. 'But why did you never come before? Mum ... ' she swallowed, 'Mum misses you so much.'

'Oh, sweetheart,' Franklin sighed, and for a moment his face looked old and tired. 'And I missed her, too. I missed both of you. But I had to remember that if I came near you, I would put you in terrible danger. The risk wasn't worth it. All that mattered to me was keeping you both safe.'

'Danger ... you mean from Angelica?'

'Yes. I knew she would try to recruit you to her cause, if she knew you existed.' He sighed. 'But turning my back on Angelica only caused more problems in the end. Maybe it was a mistake to be so harsh on her.'

'You mean ...' Sophie stopped and reached for Katy's hand. 'You mean, perhaps it's time to let the old traditions go, and for witches and witch hunters to be friends?'

Sophie's dad frowned. 'I don't know if I'd go that far. I have been in hiding from witch hunters all these years. In particular, from a family called the Gibsons, a famous and very strong witch-hunting family. They would treat you with no mercy if they found you.'

Sophie caught Katy's eye. Katy looked miserable.

'But it would be so nice to live in peace,' he said. 'To somehow call a truce with the witch hunters.'

'I'm really glad you think so, Dad,' she said, drawing Katy forward. 'Because this is my best friend, Katy ... Katy Gibson.'

Her father started, and looked at Katy in astonishment. Slowly, a smile spread over his face.

He held out a hand to Katy, who took it, blushing. He shook her hand.

'I'm very pleased to meet you,' he said.

There was a commotion in the crowd, and a figure in a black cloak and a green mask pushed her way through the people.

'Katy!' she shouted. 'Katy – I have to talk to you!'

Franklin raised his eyebrows. 'Not another witch?' he said with a smile in his voice.

Kaz reached them and pushed back her mask. She was breathless, and her eyes were reddened. 'There's been a mistake,' she burst out. Then she noticed Sophie's dad and stopped.

'Dad,' Sophie said, sensing this was not something for an adult's ears. 'Can we have a sec?'

Sophie's dad nodded and stepped away from them.

Kaz pulled Sophie and Katy in closer to her. 'I sent Callum a note asking to meet him at 9p.m. at the park. But he thought it was from you! I just signed it "K", you see.'

Sophie's mouth dropped open. So *that* was the note Callum was talking about!

'He told me he liked me ... because he thought I was you.' She hung her head.

'Oh!' Katy clapped her hands to her mouth as a smile broke over her face.

'He was so embarrassed when I took my mask off,' said Kaz, rolling her eyes. 'Katy, it's you he likes. I won't get in the way now I know that – I promise.'

Katy flung her arms round Kaz and hugged her. Kaz hugged her back.

'Well, what are you waiting for – go and find him!' Sophie laughed, giving Katy a gentle shove.

'What? Now?' she said, twisting her hair round her fingers. 'Don't you think I should—'

'Go!' Sophie and Kaz ordered together.

Katy waved and raced off through the crowd.

Kaz watched her go, with a brave smile on her face. Sophie glanced at her, wishing she could do something to make her feel better. But just then, a Jedi Knight pushed through the crowd – a Jedi Knight wearing a Grease Monkeys pin badge.

'Kaz!' Oliver tapped her on the shoulder. 'Hi. I've been looking for you.'

Kaz frowned. 'Oh yeah? Why?'

'Oh . . . I . . . Erm . . . ' Poor Oliver turned bright red.

Luckily for him Kaz had been checking out his outfit and said, 'Great badge! I *love* the Grease Monkeys.'

'Really?' Oliver said. 'Me too! Did you hear their last single? 'Meltdown'?'

'Yeah, it's so great!'

Sophie noticed Oliver taking a deep breath. 'I've got a spare ticket to their gig in December. You could come with me. You know, if you want to?'

Kaz stared at him in astonishment. 'Oliver – you're the best.' She gave him a hug, and Oliver grinned.

'If you like Grease Monkeys, you must have heard of this other band . . . '

They headed off, chatting about music.

Sophie went back to her dad who'd been standing at a little distance from them.

'Well, I can see all kinds of drama has been going on while I've been away!' he said with a smile. 'You've grown up, Sophie.'

Sophie beamed.

'I'm proud of you, sweetheart,' he said.

'Come on,' Sophie said, taking his arm. 'Let's go and find Mum.'

Sophie's dad frowned deeply. 'But the danger from the witch hunters is still very real. I wouldn't want—'

'Dad,' Sophie interrupted him, 'nothing has been worse for Mum than not having you around.'

Sophie's dad bit his bottom lip. 'I would do anything to see her again.'

'Well then,' Sophie said with a grin, 'let's do it.'

Sophie opened her garden gate. 'Here we are!'

Her father followed her through. He gazed up at the cottage, knotting his fingers together nervously. Sophie could see the sweat on his forehead.

'I don't know what I'll say to her,' he murmured.

'Just relax,' Sophie told him, smiling as she remembered giving exactly the same advice to Erin and Katy, 'and be yourself.'

'You sound as if you know what you're talking about,' he said wryly, following her down the path.

'Trust me . . . I've been doing a lot of relationship rescuing this term!'

She lifted the knocker and glanced at her father. 'Are you ready?'

Franklin took a deep breath and nodded.

Sophie hammered the knocker, and stepped back.

Her father gazed at the frosted glass panel in the door. After a long moment, Sophie saw her mother coming down the stairs.

'Sophie?' she said, her voice muffled through the door as she reached up to the latch.

Sophie's father gasped. 'I'd forgotten how beautiful her voice is,' he whispered.

Sophie's mother opened the door. 'Sophie! You're back early—' She looked up at Sophie's father, and her voice died away.

Sophie broke the silence. 'Um . . . Mum, I found . . . Dad.'

Her mother gave a sigh – and fainted.

Not exactly the reaction I was hoping for, thought Sophie, as she and her dad knelt beside her mum, fanning her face. Getting her parents back together was going to be trickier than Sophie had anticipated. But if anyone could do it, she could! She was determined . . .

Want more magic, mystery and mayhem?

The Witch of Turlingham Academy continues in:

Secrets and Sorcery